Life Story of Milarepa

Life Story of Milarepa

Tibet's Poet Saint

Ken Albertsen

Adapted from a translation from the Tibetan
by Lobsang P. Lhalungpa

BLUE DOLPHIN PUBLISHING

Published by Blue Dolphin Publishing, Inc.
P.O. Box 8, Nevada City, CA 95959
Orders: 1-800-643-0765
Web: www.bluedolphinpublishing.com

ISBN: 978-1-57733-239-8 – book only
ISBN: 978-1-57733-231-2 – book and CD
Audio version read by author.

Library of Congress Cataloging-in-Publication Data

Albertsen, Ken, 1952-
    Life story of Milarepa : Tibet's poet saint / Ken Albertsen.
        p. cm.
    "Previously published by Adventure1 Publishing, Chiang Rai,
Thailand."
    "Adapted from a translation from the Tibetan by Lobsang P.
Lhalungpa."
    ISBN 978-1-57733-239-8 (pbk. : alk. paper) —
ISBN 978-1-57733-231-2 (pbk. and cd : alk. paper)
    1. Mi-la-ras-pa, 1040-1123—Fiction. 2. Buddhist saints—Fiction.
I. Title.
    PS3601.L3349L54 2010
    813'.6—dc22
                                                                2010005526

Previously published by Adventure1 Publishing, Chiang Rai,
Thailand. Book ISBN 978-1-879338-00-5 © 2007 by Adventure1
Publications. Audio book ISBN 978-1-879338-01-2

Adapted from a translation from the Tibetan by Lobsang P.
Lhalungpa

Cover art courtesy of www.wallpapers3dvistaxp.com

Printed in the United States of America

10   9   8   7   6   5   4   3   2   1

First a Brief Introduction

M ILAREPA WAS A BUDDHIST SAINT who lived in Tibet 900 years
ago. The story takes place along the northern slopes of
the Himalayas called the Tsang, which parallels the Tsangpo
river which, in turn, flows west to east and eventually becomes the mighty Brahmaputra river.

As a boy, Milarepa was known by the name Topa-ga.
During his late teens he was referred to as "Maha-Magician"
("maha" means "great" in Sanskrit). All through the latter
part of his life he is known as Milarepa or Jetsun. This story
is based in large part upon true events in his life. Tibetans
in particular, and others who are familiar with Tibetan Buddhism, place Milarepa in an exalted status, as both a folk
hero, and a living Buddha. He stands squarely within one
of the four main pillars of Tibetan Buddhism, namely the
Kagyu lineage, which is an unbroken succession of lamas
(lama, meaning: spiritual teacher) dating from ancient times.
There are some Sanskrit and some Tibetan words peppered
throughout the story—for their brief definitions, you can go
to the addendum section.

This story also offers insights to cultural quirks of long-
ago Tibet, and to the type of Buddhism mixed with the Bon
animistic beliefs that were prevalent at that time. Some
episodes may seem outlandish, but the listener can decide
whether those parts are true-to-life depictions, or whether

they're embellishments that one might expect from centuries of re-telling a story of such epic proportions. This text does not attempt to cover the myriad details of Milarepa's life—such as naming the dozens of caves where he meditated, along with their specific locations. Nor does it try to explain the intricacies of Buddhist philosophy. Rather, it attempts to tell the story of a unique man, and the challenges in his life.

Sand mandala with blue double dorje in the middle.
Actual size is about 2 meters across.

Here Begins the Story of Milarepa

*I*N THE MIDDLE OF AUTUMN in the year of the water dragon (1052) under the star victorious of the eighth constellation in the 25th day of the moon, I was born. My father, Mila Banner of Wisdom was away in another province at the time harvesting barley. My mother, White Garland, sent him a letter which said, "I have given birth to a son. Come quickly to name him and let us celebrate his name day."

When my father received the letter, he was filled with joy and said, "Marvelous, my son has his name already. Since his birth brings me such joy, I will name him Topa-ga" (with a long o, meaning, "glad to hear" in Tibetan).

I was raised with love and heard only gentle voices of support. I was a happy child. When I was four, my mother gave birth to a girl. Peta and I were cherished children, her with long silken tresses like spun gold and me with my long shiny hair of turquoise black.

When I was about seven, my father became ill and was nearing death. Relatives and friends converged on our homestead, some traveling for days from remote valleys nestled in the northern slopes of the Himalayan range overlooking the long Tsangpo valley. All came to honor my father's passing, though some also harbored hopes of inheriting a portion of his wealth.

Father prepared a will and read to all who were assembled: "Since my son is still small, I entrust him and my property to his aunt and uncle until such time as he is old enough to take care of such affairs himself." He went on to say:

> Since I arrived in this region, I have done well for myself and my family. In the mountains we have horses, yaks and sheep. In the valley there is my field called "Fertile Triangle." There is also my large house, under which we keep cows, goats and asses. In the attic loft we have our granary plus stores of copper, iron, silver and gold—as well as turquoise gems, plus precious fabrics and silk."

> When my son is of age, let him marry his childhood sweetheart Zessay—at which time he can take possession of all that is his inheritance. During the interim period I have arranged for his aunt and uncle to take good care of him, and watch out for his sister's and his mother's well being. After I die, I will be watching all of you from the realm of the dead.

After making that proclamation, my father passed away.

A short while later, my aunt and uncle took firm control of all that was bequeathed. Very soon after that, they turned their back on promises they had made to my father. My sister, my mother and I became virtual slaves within a short time. During summers, we were required to work full-time for my uncle in the fields. During the winter when the freezing snows blew, we became full-time servants of my aunt, working long hours with wool. Our fingers became stiff with cold. When the brief days turned to night, we had to keep working by the dim light of yak butter candles.

Our food was meager and the work was strenuous. Our clothing deteriorated to tattered strips of cloth held together by bits of grass string. As we become increasingly malnourished, our once lovely tresses became matted and lice-ridden. Thus did we struggle to exist for many long years.

When I reached my fifteenth year, my mother decided to claim our full inheritance in my name. She scraped together every bit of savings and borrowed what she could in order to arrange a feast for the announcement. With white barley flour, bread and cakes were made. With black barley, beer was brewed. Animals were corralled to be slaughtered for meat. My mother and Peta even went around to borrow furniture, ornate carpets and porcelain dishes for the banquet. She invited everyone in the village, and placed my aunt and uncle at the most honored place at the table.

Near the end of the banquet, my mother stood up and loudly banged a bamboo cow bell. When she had everyone's attention, she declared, "You all know that when there is a beer fest, it is time for announcements. Well here goes. Some of you are old enough to remember the last words spoken by my husband, Mila Banner of Wisdom, at the time of his death. My son is now fifteen and of age to marry Zessay, his sweetheart. They are now old enough to have their own home." Mother then turned to face my aunt and uncle and said in a slightly wavering but loud voice, "Return the property and possessions which rightfully belong to us according to my departed husband's will. You know that's what he wanted and you know it's the right thing to do."

The aunt and uncle immediately rebuffed the idea of returning anything. They had run the manor for so many years that they had come to consider it all belonged to them. The uncle spoke tersely saying, "How can you claim to be poor? Look at this. You have prepared a lavish banquet—enough to feed the entire village. Even I could not afford such lavishness."

Brushing aside my mother's weeping, he continued, "If you are many, make war upon us. If you are few, cast spells—and see whether that will get you what you want." With those words, my aunt and uncle departed, leaving the three of us weeping on the floor. Some of the guests offered whispered words of comfort. Other guests, who worked for my uncle, offered only scowls, and ambled out of the meeting hall. Though we didn't succeed in gaining any portion of our inheritance, from that point on we ceased to be slavish servants of my aunt and uncle.

Now that we were on our own, my sister Peta did what she could to contribute. Sometimes she would "run at the sound of the bell and run when the smoke was rising," which is a Tibetan expression for showing up uninvited at monasteries or special communal events where there would be food on offer. She would quickly fill her mouth with food, while privately stuffing the pockets of her cloak with morsels to bring back home for my mother and me.

My mother was able to earn a bit by spinning and weaving wool—and in this way, she was able to send me to a lama who taught me to read and write.

One day I accompanied my lama to a ceremony. The beer was flowing like water. I got a bit tipsy and decided to head home. On the way, people were singing along the roadside, which inspired me to belt out a tune as I strolled along. I was still singing gaily as I got to the entry of my humble home. Inside, my mother was roasting barley and heard my voice.

"What is this?" she wondered, "It sounds like my son's voice, but how can he be singing when our family's plight is so miserable?"

She looked out the window and saw me in my tuneful oblivion. Her right hand dropped the spoon and her left hand dropped the whisk. She grabbed a stick in one hand and a handful of ashes in the other and strode out to confront me. The barley was left in the kitchen to burn to a powdery crisp.

Straight away, she threw the ashes in my face—blinding me with its sting, and just as quickly began striking me on the head and shoulders, all the while calling out, "Oh, Mila, my now-departed husband, is this the son you have sired!? This boy, who looks like a man, is sweetly singing while your family drowns in misery."

Peta heard the commotion and arrived upon the scene. By this time, my mother was weeping, but she continued to strike me, while wailing, "Oh Mila, he is not fit to be your son. Look at our miserable fate, mother, son and daughter!" Peta was then able to restrain my mother from beating me, and the three of us were consumed by weeping.

I pleaded to my mother, "What then should I do—I will do whatever you wish."

She said, "I sorely wish you were dressed smartly like a real man and mounted on a tall horse. I wish you had thick leather boots with sharpened stirrups, so you could gallop up to your aunt and uncle and rip open their necks. As that is not possible, I wish for you to go learn black magic so you can cast spells to destroy our enemies down to the ninth generation."

From that day, plans were set in motion for me to go study black magic and the casting of spells. I set off with some other young fellows who sought the same teachings.

Before departing, my mother took my traveling companions aside and told them that her son had no will power, so he must be spurred on to achieve all that he can. After a year of studying with a master named Yungto, my fellow students were ready to move on, but I felt I had not learned any really significant magic, other than a few spells and the mixing of some potions.

I started to depart with my friends, but then turned and returned to visit the teacher again. He asked why I had come back, and I was compelled to explain my desperate need to learn serious black magic. For the first time, I imparted the story to him of the oppression my family had suffered at my village. He listened to my story, then decided to teach me a special mantra with which I could create hailstorms. He then recommended a master in another region who could teach me incantations which cause death, and another which can cause the loss of consciousness.

I traveled again and found the respected magician he referred me to. After offering him gifts and telling my story of oppression, he agreed to be my teacher. He had me build a stone structure with no visible openings and a hidden entrance, and then he taught me the incantations.

I went inside the new structure and recited the magic mantra for seven days, and then continued for another seven days. At the end of those fourteen days, we received word that thirty-five people in my village had been seriously harmed in a dramatic fashion. They were all people who were closely associated with my aunt and uncle and had been known to contribute to my family's suffering. I later found out the details of the black magic's effect: A banquet had been held at my uncle's mansion. There were thirty-five guests inside, all members of my uncle's family and their close associates. The house suddenly shook violently and collapsed, seriously injuring all within, except my aunt and uncle who were outside fetching provisions for the party.

I found out later that when my mother heard what happened, she let out a cry of joy. She fastened a scrap of cloth to a stick and walked around waving the little banner while proclaiming, "Alas, does my deceased husband, Mila Banner of Wisdom, have a son?! Not long ago the uncle and aunt declared to us, 'If you are many, make war on us. If you are few, cast spells.' Well, this is what's been done this glorious day!"

Some of the villagers who heard her shouts of triumph thought she was justified, but felt that her revenge was too dire. They talked among themselves, saying she should be killed for her rejoicing—in response to so many peoples' injuries.

My mother got wind of the talk among the villagers, so she decided to lay low. She also got a message that I needed additional funds. She scraped together all her meager savings and was able to get hold of seven small pieces of gold to send to me. I was still far away, and there were concerns that a courier might steal whatever was sent, so she hatched a plan.

She met a wandering yogi who was headed to the region where I was studying. She invited him in for a meal, and while he relaxed at her table, she secretly took his heavy coat and placed the pieces of gold into a hidden pocket on the inside. Over the pocket she placed a patch of black cloth upon which she embroidered seven "stars" with white thread. She then gave directions to the yogi on how to find me, and handed him a sealed letter to give to me.

After the wanderer left, my mother concocted another letter and pretended that the wandering yogi had given it to her with a message from me. It read as follows:

> Dear mother, I hope you and Peta are in good health. Doubtless by now you will have seen the profound effects of the black magic I've mastered. If any surviving villagers threaten you or Peta with harm or retribution, be sure to write down their names and send the note to me. It will then be easy for me to invoke spells to harm them and their families down to the ninth generation.

My mother then fastened the contrived letter to a post in the middle of the village—for all to see.

A while later, the wandering yogi arrived at the magician's lair where I was staying. He gave me the sealed letter from my mother. I opened and read it. The letter described the details of the destruction that had taken place at our village—and how there were still many villagers who swore vengeance against our little family. In order to avert such harm against us, she advised that I enact incantations that would cause a ravaging hailstorm to rain down on the villagers' fields as high as the ninth course of bricks.

She went on to write, "If your provisions are exhausted, look to the region facing north where, against a black cloud, the constellation Pleiades appears. Beneath it you will find the seven houses of your cousins and the provisions you need. If you do not understand this part of the note, ask the wandering yogi who brings it to you. He has the cover you'll need to find your provisions."

I showed that cryptic part of the note to my master and none of us could figure out what it meant. The master's wife became curious and asked to see the note. She read it and then called for the yogi. When he arrived, she stoked the fire and gave him some beer. When he relaxed, she removed his coat and playfully put it on herself, saying, "This is a nice heavy coat for wandering the frigid slopes of these hills and valleys." She walked up to the terrace, took the coat off, examined it, then went to get a knife. She loosened the black patch on its inside lining and removed the seven gold pieces. She then got a needle and thread and re-sewed the patch as before—then went back downstairs and placed the coat on the traveler's chair.

A short while later, she gave me the gold, and I asked her why she was doing that. She replied, "Topa-ga, you have a very crafty mother. She sewed that gold in to the yogi's jacket in order to get it to you without him knowing it. The last part of your mother's letter says, 'If you do not understand this part of the note, ask the wandering yogi who bears this note. He has the cover you'll need to find your provisions.'

"The 'cover' refers to the coat that he wears. At the start of the note, she refers to, 'a region facing north,' which alludes to a place where the sun doesn't shine, in other words, the inside of the cloak. She then writes, 'look to the region facing north where, against a black cloud, the constellation Pleiades appears.' The black cloud refers to the black cloth which was used as a patch, and the seven white embroidered stars are the seven stars of Pleiades. She then writes, "Beneath it you will find the seven houses of your cousins and the provisions you need,' which alludes to the seven pieces of gold which were hidden under the patch."

The master magician overheard his wife's explanation and let out a hearty laugh while declaring, "They say women are full of guile, and it's certainly true." We all shared in his mirth.

Thus ends Chapter One.

Chapter 2

THE NEXT MORNING I gave the master magician three pieces of gold, and asked him if he would teach me the incantations for creating a shower of hailstones. He directed me to another master and gave me a letter of introduction to present to him.

I departed to the village of Kyorpa in The Yarlung region. When I found the master, I made an offering, then requested he teach me the black magic for creating hailstorms. For a week, he taught me the secret incantations, then instructed me to go within a small cell to start reciting them. On the seventh day, a miniature cloud entered the cell. Tiny shards of lightning flashed and thunder rumbled, and the voice of the maroon-faced and fearsome Dza was heard to speak. I now believed I could call forth hail with my fingertips. Every now and then the master would ask, "How high are the barley plants in your village now?"

I told him it is just starting to sprout.

A couple weeks later I told him the barley was just high enough to hide the wood pigeons.

Several weeks after that, he inquired again and I told him the barley is heavy with seed and beginning to bend.

"Then it is time to send the hailstorms," said the master.

Together with another student, both dressed as wandering monks, we set off on our mission. We hunkered down on a high hill which afforded us a faint view of the village far in the distance. The heavy heads of grain were due to be harvested the next day by a communal group of adult villagers. I started the incantations. Out of a clear sky, a little sparrow-sized cloud drifted by. I was disappointed. I threw my cloak to the ground and pleaded with the deities by their individual names. I recalled the many years my family suffered indignities by my aunt and uncle, and the same villagers who were preparing to harvest the grain. Tears of intensity streamed down my face.

Then, like a thick dark blanket, a massive black cloud began to roll in from the west. It wound up blotting out the sky and put a shadow over everything. Then a prolonged crash of thunder gave vent to sustained burst of hailstones which tore leaves from trees and scoured soil from hillsides.

The barley fields were ruined and the villagers felt a mix of sadness and anger. Sadness for all the toil in the fields that led to naught, plus no barley harvest to tide them through the winter. They were also angry at me for evoking the black magic that caused them such grief.

By harming others and being steeped in vengeful thoughts, I thus accumulated a heavy load of black karma that took many years and much effort to undo.

I returned to stay with the master magician, but soon began to feel remorse for the black deeds I had done. This created a longing within my breast for learning the purest form of dharma (spiritual path). With encouragement from the master magician, I headed off in search of a spiritual guide. During the course of my wandering, a lama was recommended. I was directed to the southern province of Lobrak and told to find the monastery of Drowo Lung. The name Lama Marpa was mentioned. The first time I heard the name Marpa, my chest swelled with happiness. Tingles of joy rippled up my back and around my body, as I knew just by hearing the name that he and I had deep karmic links going back generations. With a spring in my step, I set off for Lobrak—eagerly anticipating the moment when I would first set eyes on the lama.

I found out years later that the night before I arrived at his monastery, lama Marpa had a dream. In it, Marpa's guru, Naropa, blessed him and gave him a five-pronged vajra scepter made of gems—and also gave him a gold vase filled with nectar and said, "With the nectar in this vase wash the vajra scepter, then mount it atop the Banner of Victory peak nearby. This will please the Buddhas and make all people happy."

Still in his dream, Marpa washed the vajra and mounted it at the highest point of the Banner of Victory peak. At that moment, the vajra lit up the whole universe and liberated all classes of beings—thus filling them with bliss.

As the first light of morning lit up his room, Marpa woke from his dream and was filled with joy and happiness. A short while later Marpa's wife, named Dakmema, came in to his room bringing a cup of hot tea. Excitedly, she told him of a dream she had the night before. It involved a chorten (stupa) made from flawless crystal which needed to be cleaned and placed at the highest point. Marpa listened poker-faced as she described how the crystal then showed forth a dazzling light which infused everyone with joy. As she handed Marpa his morning tea, she asked him the meaning of the wonderful dream.

Marpa thought to himself, "Hmm, these dreams are amazingly identical and awe-inspiring." But to Dakmema he said, "I don't know the meaning of dreams, and I don't even know if dreams are such a big deal. I'm going out to plow the field near the road." Dakmema mentioned that plowing was not something befitting the high status of a lama, and suggested he get one of his apprentices to do such menial work. Marpa waved her comments aside as he took a clay pot of beer and headed off to the field. He placed the beer in a shady spot to keep it cool, then went to lazily plow while watching the road.

Meanwhile, I continued toward the direction of Lobrak Province, but no one seemed to recognize the name Marpa— until I spoke with a young boy who said that was his father's name. The boy led me to a field, and pointed to an elder man who was plowing. I felt a bit disappointed because a great teacher would not be found doing such a common chore as plowing. Perhaps the boy had misunderstood. Even so, I approached the elder field hand and said, "Pardon me, I have been told that a great lama named Marpa the Translator, disciple of Naropa, lives in this region. Have you heard of him and, if so, could you please direct me to his house?"

For a full minute the man looked at me, head to foot, then replied, "Who are you?"

I told him I was a wanderer from upper Tsang valley.

"Very well," he said, "I shall arrange for you to meet Marpa. While you're waiting, plow this field." He then took the clay pot with the beer from the spot in the ground, dusted it off and handed it to me. The beer was cool and refreshing.

"Work hard," he said as he ambled away.

I drank the beer and continued the plowing that the man had started. Near dusk, the young boy came by and said, "Come to the house. The lama will see you now." I felt great joy upon hearing this invitation.

I entered the house and saw the same elder man who had offered me the beer in the field, and I greeted him casually, wondering where the great lama was."

Then the man said, "It is evident you do not know who I am. I am Marpa; who are you? Prostrate yourself!"

I immediately bowed deeply three times at his feet, "Lama Rinpoche, I am a great sinner from Tsang region, I offer you my body, speech and mind. I ask for food, clothing and the Teaching. Please teach me the way to enlightenment in this lifetime."

The lama replied, "If you sinned, that's your business. It's not my fault. Don't be in such a hurry." He turned away to adjust an altar lamp, "What sins have you committed?"

I commenced to describe my story in detail, including the oppression my family suffered and the harsh retribution imparted by way of black magic.

The lama acknowledged my story and said, "It is good that you offer your body, speech and mind—that shows you are sincere in your quest. However, I cannot give you food and lodging as well as give you the teachings. If you choose food and lodging, then you must go to another lama to learn the teachings. If you choose the teachings, look elsewhere for food and lodging."

I replied that since I long for the teaching, I will look elsewhere for food and lodging. Even with his strict attitude, he allowed me to stay in his home for a few days.

The next day I went begging in the village and collected twenty-one measures of barley. I traded fourteen measures for a good quality metal cooking pot with four handles. I traded some of the remaining barley for a small amount of meat and beer. When I arrived at lama Marpa's house, I dropped the load of provisions on the floor. The lama immediately reprimanded me, saying, "Little man, you are a nuisance, take your things out of the entryway," and he shoved the things aside with his foot. I thought, "This man gets irritable easily, I will have to watch myself so as not to upset him."

I took the cooking pot to a water bowl and washed and dried it. A few minutes later, I approached the lama, prostrated myself, and offered him the pot. He took it in his hands and held it for a pensive moment. Tears welled in his eyes as he said, "Your gift is auspicious. I offer it to my lama, the great Naropa." He held the pot aloft and shook it, causing the four handles to clang against its sides. He then filled it with yak butter from the altar lamps. Seeing him perform this simple ritual, I was overcome with desire to learn from him. I asked him to accept me as his student.

He replied, "Disciples come to me from the regions of U and Tsang. On the way, they are attacked by brigands from Yadrok and Ling who steal their provisions and gifts. You say you are adept at manifesting hailstorms. If so, bury Yadrok and Ling with hail. After that I will instruct you."

I went to a private place and invoked the incantations. Both regions were inundated with hailstorms. Afterwards, I returned to the lama and asked for instruction.

He replied, "It is indeed true you are an adept magician, and I will name you 'Maha-Magician' ('maha' is a prefix meaning 'great'). Yet for a few hailstones, should I impart the great teachings which I brought back from India? Teachings for which I traveled long distances over high mountain passes, many times imperiling my life? Many are those who would pay gold and gems for the sacred instruction which are the living breath of the dakinis (dakinis are female angels). Now go and restore the fields and houses of Yadrok and Ling. After that I will instruct you. But if you cannot do that, leave and don't come back."

In this way the lama rebuked me and I fell to the floor in sorrow. The lama's wife came over to console me with kind words.

The next day the lama Marpa was in a pleasant mood. He came to me and said, "Last night I was quite harsh with you, but do not be distressed. Be patient. Teaching can be very slow work. Look, you are a young man with much energy, so I would like you to build a tower which I will give to my son. When you have done that, I will instruct you and will supply you with food and clothing."

I asked, "What would happen if I were to die during the construction—what then would be my fate? Would I die without ever learning religion?"

The lama replied, "I guarantee you will not die during that time. My teaching is actually expressed with few words. If you can meditate deeply according to my instructions, you will be able to attain enlightenment in your lifetime. In my Kagyu lineage, there is a powerful energy of enlightenment which is transmittable."

Upon hearing these comforting words, I was filled with joy.

Marpa had several relatives who had adjoining parcels of land. There were contentions about ownership and borders. Even so, all the relatives but Marpa had made a verbal agreement to not build fortifications on their borders. Marpa told me to build a round tower on the eastern crest, using large stones embedded in the hillside.

I toiled for a week and was half-finished when Marpa showed up and said, "The other day I had not fully considered the construction of the tower. Tear this tower down and take the stones and place them back in the hillside where you found them."

I did what he said. A while later, the lama came to me and pointed to the western crest of his property. He appeared to be drunk. He showed me a simple sketch on parchment of a semi-circular tower and said, "Make this tower over there on the crest of that hill."

So I went to work alone building the new tower. Again I rummaged around gathering large stones with which to construct walls. About halfway along, as the tower started to take shape, the lama came up to the site and said, "Its shape is not right; take this tower down and put the rocks back in the ground where you found them."

Then he took me to look at a site at the northern end of his property. He put his hand on my shoulder and said, "Maha-Magician, last week I gave you instruction to build a tower, but I was drunk at the time and did not have my wits about me. I now want you to build a sturdy tower over there on that north ridge."

I mentioned that tearing down a tower which is halfway finished is frustrating. I asked him to please think carefully before issuing instructions.

The lama responded, "Yes, you are right, but today I am not drunk and have thought about this new project carefully. The new tower will be triangular and will be called Tower of the Tantric Yogi. Build it strong. It will not be torn down."

When I was about a third of the way along with the construction, the lama walked up to the site and said, "Maha-Magician, who are you building this tower for? Who told you to build it?"

I reminded him that it was the lama himself who had told me to build it for his son.

He responded, "I do not recall giving such orders. If you are right, I must be crazy. Are you insinuating that I'm losing my mind?"

I told the lama that I suspected this might happen and re-minded him that I respectfully asked him at the time whether he was sure this was what he really wanted.

The lama asked, "Who is your witness to that conversa-tion? Perhaps you are thinking of shutting me up in your triangular tower and casting magic spells on me. I am not the one who has oppressed you and your little family and robbed you of your inheritance. If you sincerely wish for religious instruction, you should tear this tower down and return the stones to their places where you found them. After you do that, you will receive the teachings. If you don't want to do that, you may leave and not come back." Thus he spoke.

Again I obeyed, and meticulously returned the many stones to their original places on the hill. Around that time, I got a bad sore on my shoulder. It came about from repeatedly carrying heavy stones. I thought to show it to the lama, but was concerned it might arouse his anger toward me. In my pain and frustration, I decided to go and tell the lama's wife about my concerns—that I might never be given the religious instruction promised by her husband.

She went to her husband and said, "The useless toil on the towers has only brought misery to Maha-Magician. Have compassion on him and grant him the teachings he longs for."

Her husband replied, "Prepare a hearty meal and bring him to sit at my table."

When I had sat down, the lama said to me, "Maha-Magician, do not go and tattle-tale to my wife and say things about me which are not true. I have been saying you will get instruction and now I am prepared to teach."

The lama gave a teaching about the Triple Refuge and some basic tenets of Buddhism. He then told me the story of his lama, Naropa. Naropa came from the steamy valleys of India where he was known earlier as a renowned lecturer at a prestigious university. One night Naropa had a vivid dream which featured a ferocious hag which devoured everything she saw. Naropa was so moved by the dream that he decided to turn his back on his exalted status at the university, and instead strike out on his own to find a spiritual teacher. After many miles and many moons of traveling, he finally found a teacher by the side of a trail, who looked like a diminutive peasant.

Naropa's lama, Tilopa, proved to be a rare example of someone who had attained rapturous spiritual enlightenment without himself having had a guru or guide. Naropa then donned a similar tattered cloak and dedicated his spiritual quest to following everything Tilopa suggested. When Tilopa said, "If I had a real disciple, he would jump off this cliff," Naropa would immediately jump off the cliff. Tilopa would then climb down and touch Naropa and he would be healed. Another time, Tilopa said, "If I had a real disciple, he would go to that wedding celebration over there and gorge himself on food." Straightaway, Naropa strode over to the wedding, and stuffed his face with food. Within moments, the men at the party threw him out and beat him to a bloody mess. As before, Tilopa ambled over and touched him and thereby healed his wounds. By these and many other profound experiences did Naropa attain complete and blissful spiritual enlightenment for the rest of his days.

Upon hearing those gentle words from my lama, I shed tears of happiness and vowed to carry out everything lama Marpa asked of me.

Several days later, the lama took me for a walk along the south edge of his property, which bordered the properties of his jealous and untrusting cousins. The lama told me to build a large square tower and paint it white. He wanted it nine layers of stone high, with a pinnacle which could be walked-around on the uppermost deck. He said it would not be torn down and when I was finished, he would impart the secret teachings to me. Furthermore, he said I would then be allowed to go meditate in seclusion and he and his wife would provide sustenance for that period.

I agreed, but asked whether his wife, Dakmema could come to witness the promises being made. He said "fine," and called for her to join us. The lama then smoothed a section of sand on the ground, got a stick and proceeded to sketch the tower's design. The lama's wife showed up and, with him standing alongside, I declared to her, "I have already built three towers and, according to the lama's instructions, destroyed each of them in turn. Now the lama is asking that I build a fourth tower, so I am asking you to hear his promises and to be my witness."

Dakmema agreed to be a witness, but added she did not hold any real authority within the family, as the lama does much of what he wants—regardless of what others say.

Marpa then said to Dakmema, "Go ahead and bear witness. I know I will keep my word." Then he turned to me,

"Maha-Magician, if you have no faith in me or if you don't want to build the tower, then suit yourself. You are free to leave any time."

That afternoon I started laying the foundation for the tower. The next morning, while I was continuing the work, three young monks came along and playfully rolled a large rock toward the foundation and placed it as a cornerstone. A week later, as I was building the walls higher, and had just placed a heavy lintel piece over the entryway, the lama came by to inspect the progress. After pondering for a long while, he walked over and pointed a finger at the large cornerstone that had been placed by the three boys.

"Maha-Magician, where did this stone come from?"

I replied, "Three young monks come to visit several days ago and while playing around, with great effort they rolled it into place."

Marpa said, "We had an agreement that *you* were to build this tower. We had no agreement that others were going to build it. You must take that stone out and return it to where it came from."

"With all due respect sir, you promised that you would not tell me to destroy this tower."

He shot back, "I am not asking that you *destroy* the tower, but am merely saying that this stone here was not placed by you, therefore it is a breach of our agreement. I want only *this stone* taken out and returned to its place on the hillside."

For the rest of the day, I dissembled the building, stone by stone, until I was able to roll the heavy cornerstone back to its place in the ground. As the daylight was waning, Marpa showed up again and said, "All right, now you can fetch that large stone and place it back again as a cornerstone."

Thus ends Chapter Two.

Chapter 3

I RESUMED BUILDING THE TOWER. When I reached the seventh layer of stones, the sore on my back flared up worse than before—but I continued toiling.

At that time, another type of spiritual teacher called a Meton came to Marpa's compound to request a special Yidam initiation. The lama's wife said to me, "Now is an opportune time to request the Yidam teaching from Marpa."

I thought, perhaps now would indeed be a good time. I had nearly finished the nine-level tower without anyone's assistance as the lama requested. On the appointed day, I entered the inner sanctum with the others, greeted the lama, and sat down quietly in the rear of the room.

The lama came in, looked around in the candle-lit room, then he said loudly, "Maha-Magician, what gift did you bring for me?"

I told him I had fulfilled his request by building the tower for his son. I also respectfully mentioned that he had promised me initiation and instruction for doing so.

The lama responded, "You made a little tower that isn't even as thick as my arm. It is hardly a fair trade for the instruction which I brought all the way from India, with great difficulty and peril to my life. If you have the price for my teaching, then give me the payment—otherwise leave the room."

Stunned, I got up and made for the door. Just as I was about in the doorway, the lama shoved me out. I felt so dejected I wanted to die and wept the whole night. The next morning Dakmema came to console me, saying, "The lama has always said that the teachings he imparts are for the good of all beings—and he dedicates the merits of the instruction for the benefit of all. He once said that, even if a dog were to enter the room, he would teach it the doctrine. Why he refuses you, Maha-Magician, I do not know. Please don't harbor bad thoughts because of what happened."

Later that morning, the lama found me and said, "Maha-Magician, do not continue with the tower. Build a shrine at the base of it, surrounded by a covered walkway with twelve columns. When you've done that, I will give you the secret teaching."

I laid the foundation and built the covered walk. During that time, the lama's wife brought me tasty food and so much beer that I became a bit drunk. Several days later, as I was putting the finishing touches on the walkway, a lama from Dol showed up and asked for a special spiritual initiation. The lama's wife conveyed the news to me and added, "Now is a good time to ask for this special instruction."

She gave me a tub of butter, an ornate piece of cloth, and a fine copper cooking pot to give as gifts to the lama. When I entered the inner sanctum, I prostrated to the lama and offered the three gifts as payment for the instruction. Then I went to sit down with the others in attendance.

The lama asked, "Maha-Magician, what gift have you brought for me, that enables you to sit in this audience?" I respectfully replied that I had given him the butter, the cloth and the copper cooking pot.

He countered, "These are things that have been given previously by other people. Do not give me things that I already own. If you have something of your own to give me, that's acceptable. If not, leave this room now."

This time as I slunk out the door, he stood and booted me smartly in my rump. I wanted to sink into the earth. I seriously wondered if he was abusing me because of my evil deeds as a magician, and whether that marked me as never being worthy of religious instruction. I even considered suicide, thinking, "What's the use of living if I can never attain any spiritual advancement?" The lama's wife brought me a slice of the sacrificial cake, but I was too distraught to eat, and spent the whole night tossing and weeping.

The next morning the lama came by my room and said, "You are nearly finished with the tower and the covered walkway, is that not so? Go and finish those things and after that I will give you the initiation and instruction."

I spent the next week finishing the tower and the covered walkway. By that time, my back had become a mass of infected sores. My shirt was stained red and yellow from blood and pus. I showed my sores to Dakmema and begged her to assist me with getting her husband to impart the spiritual instruction—and to remind him of all the promises he had made over time. When she saw the sores, her eyes welled up with tears. She told me she would go and speak to him.

She addressed Marpa, "You are known far and wide by the exalted title Lama Rinpoche. Yet you cause Maha-Magician to work like a slave. On his back are three large infected sores. I might expect to see such sores on a beast of burden but certainly never on a person. I am ashamed to be the wife of someone who causes such pain—especially a renowned lama as yourself. Maha-Magician is worthy of instruction. You have been telling him you would impart the higher teachings, but you have not. Has he not built the tower you told him to build?"

Marpa replied, "He has appeared to have built the tower. Are the sores really so bad? Bring him to me so I can see for myself."

When I arrived, the lama asked me to remove my shirt and show him my back.

After a few moments of examination he said, "My guru Naropa underwent twenty-four mortifications of the flesh, twelve great and twelve minor trials—all severe tests of his commitment—any one of which was more dire than the sum of the trials you have suffered at this compound. As for me, I nearly sacrificed my life traveling to, and returning from India in my quest to seek the divine instructions from Naropa. If you, Maha-Magician, seek the teaching, be humble and continue to work on finishing the tower as we agreed."

Having said that, he instructed his wife to clean my sores, while he took a pillow and fashioned a pad to protect my wounds from the heavy stones I would carry. He also suggested, rather than carrying earth and mortar in a bundled cloth upon my shoulders, it would be better to carry such things in a clay pot carried in front. I found out later, that when the lama observed me working alone so diligently, according to his instructions, he privately shed tears of compassion for me.

Despite the added bit of concern, my sores became worse and I was bedridden with fever. The lama's wife helped me gain some strength with food and drink, then asked Marpa to allow me to continue to rest and recuperate. However, when the lama saw I could sit up in bed, he insisted I was strong enough to get back to work on the tower.

I was preparing to go back to work, when the lama's wife approached me in private to hatch a plan which would enable me to get the teachings. She had me pack my magic book and my few possessions in a bag, plus a small sack of flour—and pretend I was leaving the compound altogether. As I departed, she pretended to be pleading for me to stay, calling out, "Please don't go away. If you ask the lama, he will give you the instruction, despite all that's happened thus far."

Marpa witnessed the commotion and asked what was going on.

Dakmema reminded him of the details of how I came to this place seeking the teachings, yet have thus far only suffered disappointments. The lama became angry and walked briskly out to me and began slapping me like I was a very naughty boy, saying, "When you came here, you said you would give me your body, speech and mind. In so doing, you made a pledge to belong to me. Surely you are not leaving now? I own you, and could cut you to pieces like a goat being prepared for a banquet soup." He slapped me a few more times, then grabbed the sack I was holding and said, "This flour belongs to me"—then marched back to his house with it.

My whole body shook with misery. My despair was like a boy who has lost his whole family in a rock slide. The next day Dakmema came to console me. She decided to impart spiritual instruction that she was familiar with. She taught me the method for meditating on Dorje Pagmo. It was beneficial and lifted my spirits a bit. I became like a child, helping her with daily chores. When she milked cows, I would hold the bucket for her. When she roasted barley grain, I held the pan for her. Gradually I thought more and more of finding another teacher, but I doubted whether any other lama had quite the depth of spiritual attainment as Marpa. As I continued thinking about moving elsewhere, I went back to work putting the finishing touches on the tower.

As I was mixing mortar to stucco the outside walls, a lama from another monastery named Shung passed by with a small group of monks. They had numerous presents and I asked them where they were going. They told me they were going to ask lama Marpa to impart the great initiation of Hevajra—the demon-like deity who can be transformed to a protector by intense meditation and ritual.

The lama's wife got wind of what was going on and came to me. For years she had a large turquoise pendant that she had received from her family, and which she had kept in a private hideaway, so not even her husband knew about it. She passed it to me and suggested I use it as a gift to the lama in hopes of getting the sacred instruction.

All the guests had prostrated and given their gifts to the lama and went to find a place to sit in the inner sanctum. I was in line as well, and when it came my turn, I offered the impressive turquoise pedant to him. As I stood there, the lama turned it over in his hands, pondering its beauty. He asked where I got it. As I could not lie to my lama, I told him that Dakmema gave it to me. The lama cracked a wry smile, and asked me to go and get her.

When she arrived, he asked her where the pendant came from.

She replied, "I don't need to tell you, but I'll tell you anyway. When I was about to marry you, my parents knew you had a terrible temper. Out of concern for their daughter, they secretly gave me this turquoise. The idea being, if we should ever divorce, I would have something of value with which to pick up the pieces and start a new life. It is mine and I chose to give it to Maha-Magician for whom I feel profound pity. Marpa, just accept it and grant the initiation to the young man. Hasn't he suffered enough?" When she finished, she prostrated to her husband over and over. Several times she turned to compel the others in the room to join her in her prostrations to implore Marpa to have pity, but the others assembled were so struck by Marpa's now terrifying countenance, that they froze in place.

Finally Marpa spoke. "Through the kindness of my wife, this valuable pendant nearly became the possession of a stranger." Then, tying it around his neck, he went on, "Wife, do you not know that whatever you brought in to the marriage becomes mine?" Then turning to me he said, "Maha-Magician, do not give me a gift that I already own. If you have something of value, give it to me. If you have nothing of your own to offer, then leave this room."

Thinking that Dakmema would continue her pleadings on my behalf, I remained for a moment in my place. But the lama's anger erupted. He jumped up, grabbed me by the ear and roughly forced me out the door—where I fell and bumped my head on the stone floor.

Marpa went back inside, but Dakmema came out and stroked my head saying, "Maha-Magician, please don't be too distressed. We did all we could do. If you want to go to study with another lama, I will help you get whatever you need to break away from here." I felt so bad, I wished I could be sucked in to the stone floor to die.

The next morning the lama summoned me. When I arrived, he asked in a calm voice whether I was dissatisfied, or whether I harbored any evil thoughts toward him.

I told him I had faith in him, and had never uttered a word of rebellion or had a thought of retribution towards him. I went on to acknowledge that I had accrued much black energy from the evil deeds I had done as a practitioner of black magic—and any misery I feel now, has been brought on by myself. Then I wept. Marpa's voice then waxed firm as he said, "What do you expect to gain from all these tears of self-pity? Be gone. Get out of here."

I was now confused. I thought about the time when I had the money my mother had sent me. If I had used that gold to offer to a spiritual teacher instead of a master magician, then perhaps I would have made some headway here at Marpa's compound. As it stood now, I could not afford to offer any real gifts to Marpa. The same predicament would befall me if I were to go to another lama—because all through Tibet it is known, if a student approaches a teacher to gain instruction, it is imperative that something of value be offered as a gift.

I thought about serving a rich man or perhaps going to a village to earn wages to save up in order to afford instruction.

I decided I must either find a lama who would instruct me without requiring gifts, or else search for a way to work to earn some savings.

The next morning I departed without even saying good-bye to the lama or his wife. I found out later that soon after I left, the lama's wife had entered his chamber and said to him, "There now, the great annoyance in your life has finally left. It is surprising he did not leave a lot sooner. Now you can relax without him disrupting your life any more. He's gone for good."

The lama asked, "Who has gone?"

She replied, "Who but Maha-Magician has been a thorn in your side? You treat him like dirt, you embarrass him in front of others, you abuse him every chance you get. Now he's gone and you can rest easy."

Upon hearing that, the lama's eyes welled up with tears. He looked up at the ceiling and called out mournfully, "La-mas of the Kagyu order, Dakinis, and protectors of religion— bring back my pre-destined son!" He then wrapped his maroon cloak around his head and body, and sat motionless for a long time.

When I secretly left that morning, I didn't even take a small sack of barley flour for fear of angering the lama. After a trek of several hours, I grew hungry and stopped to beg for some tsampa.

I borrowed a pot and made a small fire in order to cook the grain. I realized the effort needed to make just one little meal and it filled me with appreciation for the lama's wife who cooked a meal for me every day. And I didn't even have the courtesy to say good-bye when I left. I thought of going back, but did not have the courage. When I returned the cooking pot, a well-to-do villager said to me, "Young man, you seem fit enough to work. Rather than beg, why not go in to homes and recite prayers—if you know how to read."

I told him I was not a common beggar and that I did know how to read. He said, "All right, you can start at my house. I will pay you well to recite prayers for the prosperity and well-being of my family." I stayed there for a while and received wages for recitations. During my spare time I was able to read religious books from my host's library. I read The Eight Thousand Stanzas and also a book about Taktugna who was a sensitive saint who wept at the slightest hint of joy or sorrow. I thought about how he also had no money nor gifts to offer for teachings, yet he would have torn out his heart and sold it if it could have furthered his quest for enlightenment. Compared to his commitment, I look like a lightweight. I realized then, that there still might be a chance that Marpa would impart his teachings to me—if I would merely show my sincere intent on attaining enlightenment in this life. After contemplating the deep sacrifices of others, I started back on the trail to lama Marpa.

When I returned to Marpa's place, Dakmema came out joyously to greet me, saying, "Here you are at last! The lama will surely teach you now. When I told him you had left, he was saddened by the news and called you his pre-destined son."

I thought that maybe Dakmema had misconstrued the words and instead the lama had simply said, "Bring him back to me." I did not want to get my hopes up too high—with the possibility they'd be dashed, as had happened so many times before.

I had an audience with lama, where he said I had forsaken him and the family by slinking away without even saying goodbye. He said if I really wanted the teachings, I would have to construct a roofed walkway to go around the existing tower. He said if I did that, I could receive the teachings. Otherwise, it was costly to feed me and if I had somewhere else to go, then I had better be on my way.

I surmised that the same pattern might be repeated, where I would be promised the teaching for doing construction, and then be refused later on. I did not express this to the lama, but I did mention it to his wife. She agreed, and reminded me of a plan she had mentioned earlier—for me to go and study with an affiliated lama in Shung named Ngokpa who had a small monastery in a neighboring valley. To facilitate my acceptance there, Dakmema had secretly taken a couple precious items from lama Marpa's altar—in fact, they were precious jewels received from Naropa plus a rosary of rubies. She handed me the items, plus a forged letter of recommendation from Marpa—to use as offerings to the other lama.

Thus ends Chapter Three.

Chapter 4

I SET OFF FOR SHUNG. After a two day trek I rounded the crest of a steep hill leading to the monastery. I saw a group of monks sitting with a teacher in the distance. Lama Ngokpa was reading aloud from a religious text, the following words, "I am master of the Dharma, I am master of the universe and the object of realization. I am the innate nature of spontaneous bliss."

As he said that verse, he looked up and saw someone in the distance, prostrating toward their gathering. He removed his arched hat and said, "This manner of greeting is used by Marpa's disciples. And it is a good omen that he caught my notice just as I was reading those auspicious words. This man could be destined to be the master of all doctrines. Someone go ask him who he is."

A boy came up the hill and recognized me from an earlier visit to Marpa's. I told him of the gifts and the letter I carried. He raced down the hill and informed the others. When lama Ngokpa heard, he rejoiced at the good fortune of receiving the Naropa jewels and the ruby rosary. He asked to see the letter and read it out loud: "To lama Ngokpa, Since I have gone in to seclusion, and Maha-Magician lacks patience, I am sending him to you for the teaching. Give him initiation and instruction. I hope you appreciated the jewels of Naropa and the ruby rosary."

Lama Ngokpa was glad to have me as a part of his group. My reputation as a magician had preceded me, and as a preliminary condition of acceptance, he asked that I perform some black magic. He told me bad people from outlying villages had robbed monks who had been traveling through their regions. He requested that I send hailstorms to destroy their fields and houses. Though I had hoped to never again perform black magic, I felt obligated to please my new lama. I gathered together some ritual objects and infused some sesame seeds with magic power. I then went to a hillside near the villages to be destroyed, and started the incantations.

As dark storm clouds began gathering, an old woman happened by and noticed my ritual. She quickly realized what I was doing, and implored me to spare her fields, otherwise she would have nothing to eat for the coming winter. It made me realize what a bad thing I was doing. I asked her to quickly draw an outline in the sand of the shape of her field. She drew a long triangular shape. I cupped my hands in the form of a mudra and placed them above the drawing on the ground. My hands were unable to cover one corner of the drawing. A while later, I went to observe the aftermath of the devastation. Hillsides were denuded, crops were flattened, roofs of homes were blown away. All alone, unscathed, was the triangular-shaped field belonging to the old woman, except for one corner which was eroded away—the one corner on the drawing which my hands had not been able to cover.

On my return to the lama Ngokpa, I saw two shepherds and told them it was I who had brought black magic upon their region. I admonished them to no longer harass the students of lama Ngokpa—for this will be their retribution. Further on, I noticed dozens of dead birds, reptiles and rodents along the path. I bent down to pick them up and placed them in a fold made from my cloak.

When I returned, I dumped the dead animals in front of the main room. I explained to lama Ngokpa that I had been a great sinner and that I no longer wanted to perform black magic. He understood and consoled me. He acknowledged the pile of dead animals and it inspired him to quote from a sutra called "driving away a hundred birds with a single pebble from a slingshot"—which enables sinners to attain enlightenment instantly. He assured me that in the future, all the dead animals would be reborn in higher realms. He then snapped his fingers, and one by one the creatures revived— some flying off and others scurrying away.

That evening, lama Ngokpa gave me initiation into the mandala of Hevajra, one of the primary demons who, through ritual, can be made into a protector for those seeking spiritual development. After that teaching, I moved in to an abandoned cave on a cliff facing south. I walled it in, leaving a small opening through which the lama could impart instruction. I meditated intensely, but because I had left my primary lama, Marpa, without permission, I had no deep visions. A while later lama Ngokpa asked whether I had experienced any profound insights, and I replied that I had not.

He was perplexed and wondered whether something was wrong with the transference of spiritual energy inherent within the Kagyu lineage, or whether there was a flaw in his teaching or the doctrine itself.

Some time later, lama Ngokpa received a letter from lama Marpa which read as follows: "You and your fellow monks are invited to the consecration of my son's newly completed tower. We will have a celebration day. Bring also a certain evil-doer who belongs to me."

Lama Ngokpa immediately realized what he had suspected for a while. He knew the stormy history between Marpa and me. He brought the letter to the opening at my cave and read it to me. "You are the evil-doer referred to in this letter, are you not?" he said.

I then told him the full truth; that I had arrived with a false letter and that the gifts I offered were not really mine to give. It was clear then, that the reason my meditations were not revealing any deep insights was because I had come to study with Ngokpa by way of false pretenses. Ngokpa and I agreed that we would travel together to the consecration ceremony, though I would go as Ngokpa's servant rather than his student. In the meantime it was decided I should stay in seclusion.

A week before the consecration date, a servant was sent ahead to Marpa's compound to finalize preparations. When he returned to Ngokpa's place, he came to my cave and handed me a small gift from Marpa's wife, Dakmema. It was a clay die used for games and gambling. I was in a playful mood, so I tossed the die to and fro. I thought it was a strange gift since the lama's wife knew I never played dice nor gambled—indeed it was a rather cheap gift and I thought maybe this was an indication that she didn't much care for me anymore.

I tossed the die up to the roof of the cave and, in the dim light, I missed it coming down and it fell and broke on the floor. Out tumbled a small roll of paper which I took to the waning light at the cave's opening. It read, "Now the lama will surely initiate you and give you the teaching. Return with lama Ngokpa." Reading it gave me such joy that I jumped from side to side in the cave like a madman.

The next day, preparations were made to travel to the celebration. Lama Ngokpa wanted to make a good impression, so for gifts, he gathered up a veritable treasure of ornate cloth, silk, and gems. He also arranged for all the goats at his compound to be herded along for the meat and milk they would add to the festivities. Only one animal, an old goat with a broken foot, was left behind. Ngokpa passed a bag of cheese, some silk cloth and a polished opal gem to me to use as offerings to lama Marpa.

As we neared the approach to the valley where Marpa's compound was located, Ngokpa asked for me to go ahead of the procession in order to request some beer be sent back for the thirsty travelers. At the edge of the property I was met by the lama's wife. We joyfully greeted each other and I gave her the bag of goat's cheese. I told her lama Ngokpa will soon be arriving and relayed his request for beer to be sent. She said, "Marpa is at the house; he should be glad to see you; go ask him yourself."

I found Marpa on his terrace looking pensive. I prostrated and offered him the silk and opal. He turned his head away. I repositioned to face him and again I prostrated, but he turned again to face away from me.

I said, "Oh master, is it right that you should shun me and my offerings? Lama Ngokpa will soon arrive with a veritable treasure trove of gifts to offer you. He is only requesting that someone will receive him now with some refreshment."

Marpa then came alive with a profound and terrible voice, "From the three collections of sacred books, I extracted the essence of the four tantras. I traveled hundreds of miles through treacherous territory—risking my dear life to bring the sacred teachings of Vajrayana to Tibet. At one point, half-way back on my journey, my traveling companion argued ineffectually with me. In his anger at debating with a superior thinker, he flew in to a rage and tossed all my precious books from a bridge in to a raging river. I then had to return to India to retrieve what I could. When I finally returned to Tibet from my arduous journey, no one came to greet me, not even a little bird. Now, because Ngokpa is arriving, pushing a few debilitated goats before him, he demands that I, the great Translator, should get up and go greet him. I shall not—now get out of my sight!" Thus spoke Marpa.

Now chastened to my sandals, I left to inform the lama's wife and together we returned to greet Ngokpa and his growing entourage. Many villagers had been drawn to join the assembly, as the news spread quickly that there was about to be a ceremony and banquet to consecrate the new tower.

When Marpa looked out and saw the mass of people, his mood brightened. In his booming baritone voice he sang a chant of thanksgiving for the occasion:

> I call upon my master Naropa, the compassionate One. Excellence abounds in this precious lineage of mine, unstained by flaw or deficiency.

> May all be blessed through this excellence. Excellence abounds in the rapid path of secret transmission. Without error or deception.

May all be blessed through his excellence. Excellence abounds in Marpa the Translator guarding the essence of these secrets.

May all be blessed through his excellence. Excellence abounds in lamas, yidams and dakinis possessing the power of blessing and true realization.

May all be blessed through this excellence. Excellence abounds in the spiritual disciples assembled in your faith and in your vows.

May all be blessed through this excellence. Excellence abounds in benefactors near and far, accumulating merit through their generosity.

May all be blessed by way of this excellence. Excellence abounds in multiple protective deities remaining faithful to their sacred pledges.

May all be blessed through his excellence. Excellence abounds in monks and lay people assembled here today. In their aspiration for peace and happiness, may all be blessed through his excellence.

Thus chanted Marpa. Then lama Ngokpa offered him the multitude of gifts saying, "Lama Rinpoche, herein I offer all my worldly goods, except one decrepit goat with a lame foot who was not able to keep up with the herd. Respectfully I ask that you grant us the initiation and profound instruction written on the holy scrolls which are safeguarded in your care."

Lama Marpa responded, "Yes, it is true that I possess the holy scrolls which contain the sacred teachings of Vajrayana, which describe the shortest path to attaining enlightenment in this life. And it is true that the scrolls are kept under tightest security as mandated by my lama Naropa, the dakinis and other guardian deities. For that reason, I will not be able to impart the teachings without also receiving the old goat with the broken foot."

Everyone broke in to laughter. Then lama Ngokpa's voice rose above the crowd, "Does that mean if we bring the old goat here as an offering, that you will reveal the sacred teaching?"

Marpa answered, "If you bring the goat yourself, and offer it to me, then yes, you and your students can have the teaching."

The next day Ngokpa set off to retrieve the old goat, and returned that evening with it straddled on his shoulders. When he offered it to Marpa, the master announced joyfully, "Ngokpa, you are an initiated disciple worthy to be called faithful to his sacred bond. I have no need for this goat. I only wanted to stress the importance of giving all you have to give."

Later that evening, as everyone was gathered around a fine feast, Marpa, with a stout stick by his side, asked Ngokpa why he had given initiation and instruction to the evil-doer known as Maha-Magician.

Lama Ngokpa prostrated himself and said, "Lama Rinpoche, I was led to believe that you yourself wrote and asked that I initiate and instruct Maha-Magician. Besides the sealed letter, I received the gifts of Naropa's jewels and the rosary made from rubies. Thus I thought I was carrying out your express wishes."

There was a long silence. Everyone's gaze was fixed upon Marpa, as his face became suddenly very stern in the candle-light. He turned his head slowly to me and asked where I got Naropa's jewels and the ruby rosary.

My heart agonized as if it had been torn out. I was mute with terror. In a trembling voice I told Marpa that those items had been given to me by his wife, Dakmema.

Immediately, Marpa grabbed the stick, rose up and sought out his wife to give her a beating. Sitting nearby, she too stood up quickly and ran away. She knew the altar room was the one lockable place in the house, so she ran directly there and locked herself in. The lama got to the door, shook it, then returned to sit down with the others. He then turned and told Ngokpa that he acted outside his authority, and to go right away to retrieve Naropa's jewels and the ruby rosary and return them. Marpa then covered his body and head with his maroon robe and sat motionless for a long time. Lama Ngopka prostrated three times before Marpa, then prepared to go back to his compound to retrieve Naropa's jewels and the rosary.

I felt truly miserable. Thinking this scenario was the death knell for any chances I might have had for gaining enlightenment, I seriously contemplated suicide. I went to the kitchen to get a knife. Ngopka saw the seriousness of the situation and came in to restrain me. With tears in his eyes he told me, "According to the teachings of the Buddha, each person has the potential to attain enlightenment, therefore each person is innately divine. Killing yourself is akin to killing a deity. Maha-Magician, I have met many seekers in my time, and you have great potential for attaining enlightenment in your lifetime. There is no one I know who is better suited." Thus spoke Lama Ngopka.

I called out in anguish, "Oh, lama Ngopka, my heart must be made of iron, for if not, it would surely have burst by now! Certainly lama Marpa would never even consider granting me the secret teaching—after what just happened."

Ngopka said, "Not to worry. Though I still believe there's a chance Marpa will grant you the instruction, even if he doesn't, another lama will. If he refuses you, then it is the same as if he releases you from his tutelage—so you would therefore be free to seek refuge with another lama."

Students were milling between the locked shrine room, the kitchen and the main room. They would listen to bits of conversation between me and Ngopka, and then return to the main room, where they would prostrate before the shrouded lama Marpa. With tears in their eyes they fervently pleaded for him to have mercy upon Dakmema and show forgiveness for me.

A while later, Marpa unwrapped the cloak from his head and he appeared calm. He asked why everyone was milling aimlessly around the house. He was told that Ngokpa was about to leave to retrieve Naropa's jewels and the ruby rosary, but had chosen to stay close to Maha-Magician for fear he might commit suicide.

Marpa said he wasn't worried about getting Naropa's jewels and the rosary right away, and trusted those things would be returned soon. In a calm and clear voice, he called for Dakmema and everyone else to come together again in the main room.

I heard the summons but refrained from returning, afraid that Marpa would do his customary rebuke and make me feel like the least piece of dirt. Sensing my depression, Ngopka chose to stay in the kitchen by my side.

Dakmema sheepishly returned to the main room. Marpa asked why Maha-Magician was not in attendance. A young monk spoke up, and explained the dramatic scenario which was taking place in the kitchen, and how I was wary about returning to join with everyone else in Marpa's presence.

Marpa responded, "Ordinarily, he would be right to shy away from joining us, but today I will not act harshly as I have before. Maha-Magician is to be the guest of honor; let my wife go and fetch him."

Dakmema, both joyful and fearful, came to tell me, "Marpa now appears ready to take you as a disciple. He appears to be level-headed and compassionate, like I've rarely seen him. He even said that you are to be the guest of honor. Come on, he asked me to fetch you. This looks like the real thing this time." She smiled and led me in.

Thus ends Chapter Four.

Chapter 5

MARPA ADDRESSED those assembled in his room, "If everything is looked at objectively, you'll see that no one is to be blamed for anything that's taken place. These long months, I have had to subject Maha-Magician to great tribulations, in order to purify him of his sins. I had to break down his magician's ego, in order to enable him to be able to accept the religious teachings. My wife didn't know about this plan, and it was only natural that she acted with kindness and compassion, as is her nature—however she nearly went out of bounds by giving away the precious relics and forging the note from me. Ngopka did nothing wrong, though when I finish speaking, he should go get the sacred objects and bring them to me. Afterwards I will give them to him properly.

"You have all seen me get angry; some of you have seen it repeatedly in recent months. It was anger like rising floodwater, not like worldly anger. Strange as it may seem, all my actions, even the anger, were in line with higher doctrine and were spiritually motivated.

"The past sins of Maha-Magician have been erased by his sufferings here. I have loved him as though he were my dearest son. Maha-Magician, you have been, and continue to be, as dear to me as my own heart. I accept you as my disciple and will give you my teaching. You will be provided with provisions and be allowed to meditate and be happy." Thus spoke Marpa.

Marpa the Translator

I was hearing the words spoken by lama Marpa, but wasn't sure whether I was in a lovely dream. If this was a dream, I didn't want to be awoken. I looked around at the others and realized this was for real. My body felt tingles of exhilaration, and tears of joy coursed down my cheeks.

A ritual feast was arranged and after nightfall, we all assembled near the altar. Marpa said to me, "I ordain you with the vow of liberation." He then cut off my long hair.

I changed in to a monk's robe and the lama said, "I ordain you with the name Mila Vajra Banner of Victory. That name was revealed to me by Naropa in a dream—even before you came here."

He then consecrated the holy wine in a skullcap, and we all saw it bubbling with the luminescence of five colors. He made an offering to Naropa and to the yidam, then he drank the first sip. He handed the skullcap to me and I drank the rest.

Our eyes met and he said, "Drinking all the remaining wine is a good omen. A mere taste of the consecrated wine is, in itself, superior to receiving the complete initiation of any other lineage. Starting tomorrow, I shall teach you 'the initiation of transformation according to the secret path.'" Thus he spoke.

During this time, elder monks had been making an elaborate mandala on the floor, using many different colors of sand, precisely placed in detail. Marpa took us to view it, and said, "Behold the Chakrasamvara mandala with sixty-two deities. It is beautifully elaborate, but is just colored sand." He then pointed skyward and said, "The real mandala is up there."

We all looked up at the evening sky, and could clearly make out details of the same Chakrasamvara mandala on a cosmic scale. We saw it surrounded by dakas and dakinis of the twenty-four sacred realms; we saw the thirty-two charged sites, and the eight great places of cremation. Some of us saw the mandala in multiple dimensions.

Lama Marpa gave me the recitation of Tantra teachings. Then, placing his hands gently on my head, he said, "My son, the night before you first came to this place, I was shown in a dream that you were destined to serve the teachings of the Buddha. My wife had a similar dream the same night—which saw two women guardians of a chorten indicating that the dakinis will protect the teaching of our lineage. When we first met, I made like a laborer plowing the field. You drank all the beer I offered. By doing that, and finishing plowing the field, you signified that you will penetrate to the heart of the doctrine and you will grasp the divine essence of the entire teaching.

"The copper pot with the four handles, that you offered me that evening, signified that your mind will become crystal clear from blemish and your body will attain the fire of Tummo—which is the blissful attainment of spiritual heat."

Still with his hands placed gently on my head, the lama continued, "The emptiness of the pot foretold the paucity of food during your upcoming times of meditating in solitude. I clanged the pot and it rang with a clear tone, which presaged your future renown. I filled the pot with clarified butter for the well-being of your many future disciples and to ensure that you infuse them with the sweetness of the teachings. The difficult toil of building the towers was a means to purify you from the darkness of evil you had accrued from practicing black magic.

"Each time I chastised you and drove you out from the ranks of the other disciples, you were overwhelmed with grief, but you had no bad thoughts against me personally. That signifies that your future disciples will have boundless zeal, perseverance, and compassion. Because your disciples will not crave material wealth, they will have a great capacity to persevere with their meditations in the mountains. Their ascetic discipline and energy will be exemplary. The transmission of this teaching will be as inevitable as the waxing moon, so rejoice!" Thus spoke lama Marpa.

The next day, preparations were set in motion for me to go into meditation retreat. Marpa directed me to a secluded cave called Tiger Nak. I gathered rocks, and sealed off most of the opening, then went in and found a good spot to sit. I filled a small altar lamp with yak butter, lit it, and placed it by my head. For several days and nights I meditated without moving, until the lamp went out. I continued meditating in the cave for many months, during which a monk appointed by the lama would bring me modest food and water—and set it at the cave opening.

After eleven months, lama Marpa and his wife showed up one morning and brought food from a ritual feast. He said, "Well, my son, to meditate in seclusion for eleven months without letting your cushion get cold is excellent. Remove some rocks and return home to rest so that we may talk, father and son, about your inner revelations."

It felt odd to leave the cave, as I had become accustomed to its seclusion. The lama and Dakmema departed. As I removed rocks from the entry and allowed the sun to stream in, I paused. It was too much sensory input all at once, after sitting in a dark cave for so long. I must have hesitated a long time, because Dakmema returned at dusk to gently persuade me to come out and return to the house.

After cleaning up, I joined the lama in his altar room. With a gentle voice he asked that we commune together. Then he asked me to relax and tell what spiritual insights I had experienced during my meditations in seclusion. With great veneration toward the lama, I knelt down and joined

my hands together in a prayer-like mudra. With tears well-
ing in my eyes, I paid homage to him and sang a song of the
Sevenfold Devotions:

> Oh Master, who, to the eyes of impure seekers appears in
> diverse forms, and to the assembly of pure Bodhisat-
> tvas manifesting as Buddhas, I bow to you.

> Sounding the sixty tones of celestial Brahma, you spoke
> about the sacred teaching in its eighty-four thousand
> aspects, which was understood by people, each in
> their own language. I prostrate myself before your
> speech, which is inseparable from emptiness.

> In the clear and lucid space of Dharmakaya, there is no
> defilement of discrimination, yet it encompasses all
> knowledge. I bow to the immutable Dharmakaya.

> Dwelling in the place of pure emptiness, revered Dakme-
> ma, with glowing body, you are the mother who bears
> the Buddhas of the Three Ages. Mother Dakmema, I
> prostrate myself at your feet.

> Master Marpa, with great respect, I bow to your spiritual
> sons who will spread the doctrine, and I bow to your
> many followers. I offer my body to you, and whatever
> else I can offer which is worthy of sacrifice.

> I repent all my sins, one by one. I delight in the virtuous
> deeds of others. I implore you to turn the Wheel of
> Dharma far and wide.

> I pray that the lama may live, so long as there are sentient
> beings entangled in samsara. May my spiritual merits
> and achievements benefit all beings.

> Great lama, who is the Buddha Vajrahara, and Mother
> Dakmema, bearer of Buddhas, please hear me out; you

have patiently put up with my faults, my ignorance, and my errors, and have corrected them according to the Dharma and for this I will be ever appreciative.

Under the glorious rays emanating from the sun of your compassion, the lotus of my mind has opened. May the fruits of my meditation be beneficial to all beings.

Thus I spoke.

Lama Marpa, radiant with joy, then spoke, "My son, I had great hopes for you and my hopes have been realized."

A short while later, I returned to the cave and again walled up the entrance. One night, a dakini appeared to me. She was in the form of a beautiful girl, blue as the sky. She had a brocade dress and shiny bone ornaments that hung about her neck, wrists and ankles. Her eyebrows and lashes sparkled with light. She spoke to me saying, "Dear one, you have received several esoteric teachings which lead to supreme enlightenment, but you have not received the tantric teaching called 'Transference of Consciousness to Dead Bodies'—which can lead to Buddha consciousness in one meditation sitting. Ask for it," she said, then suddenly disappeared.

I realized this was a specific message from the realm of the dakinis, and felt it was important to go to lama Marpa and ask him about this doctrine.

I broke an opening in the cave and went down to visit with the lama. He was not pleasantly surprised, and asked what was so important, that I had to prematurely break my seclusion.

I told him of my vision with the dakini and her message regarding the "Transference of Consciousness to Dead Bodies." Marpa recollected, though there had been a mention of that when he was with Naropa, he could not recall whether he had asked his guru for that specific instruction, as there had been so many teachings during that time. The lama and I searched day and night through his many religious texts, and though we found several mentions of transference of consciousness, we did not find any that specifically mentioned such transference to dead bodies. In conclusion, Marpa decided to make the long trek back to India to ask Naropa for the teaching. I reminded him he was no spring chicken any more, but nevertheless, he converted his possessions in to gold and set off for the steamy plains of India.

When Marpa arrived, he found that Naropa was out traveling. He finally caught up with Naropa at a forest retreat and asked for instruction for "Transference of Consciousness to Dead Bodies."

Master Naropa asked, "Did you think of this, or did you receive a sign."

Marpa replied that one of his young disciples named Topa-ga had received the message from a dakini.

"How marvelous!" exclaimed Naropa. He then joined his hands above his head, and with a radiant smile, he looked skyward and chanted, "Oh, disciple called Topa-ga, I prostrate myself before you. You are like the sun rising on the snow in the shadows of the somber north. The bright light of your radiance will illuminate every dark corner of the world." Naropa then faced north and bowed three times toward Tibet. Soon after, he imparted the secret teaching to

*A depiction of some dakinis—though they're usually depicted
with bluish skin tone*

Marpa—then the lama embarked on the long journey back to Tibet.

When he arrived back home, we arranged for a ritual meal. Marpa and his four chief disciples were assembled. One asked, how will the Kagyu lineage continue when the lama passes away, and what are the individual dharmas for his chief disciples? Marpa said he had the power to interpret dreams, and encouraged his disciples to meditate, and then describe their dreams in detail the following morning. The other disciples had inspiring dreams. I was last to speak and I described my dream of the Four Pillars:

> I dreamed in the vast north a majestic snow-covered mountain arose, its white peak touching the sky. Around it turned the sun and moon, the light filling the whole of space, and its base covered the entire Earth. Rivers flowed down its sides to the four directions, quenching the thirst of all beings. The waters rushed on, to empty into the sea. Countless flowers sparkled along its route.

> I dreamed that on the east side of the mountain a great pillar arose. At the top crouched a great snow leopard, his mane flowing regally. He spread his claws upon the snow and gazed upward, then roamed proudly on the vast snow pack.

> I dreamed that to the south a great pillar arose, at the top a tigress roared. Multi-colored hair covered her body. She smiled three times while spreading her claws over the forest. Her eyes gazed upward while she walked regally above the jungle.

> I dreamed that in the west a great pillar arose and at its peak sat a giant garuda bird. It spread its wings and dropped off to soar majestically around the apex of the pillar. With its eyes gazing upwards, it slowly gained altitude with the upswell from below.

I dreamed that to the north, a great pillar was raised and at its top stood an imposing vulture. It spread its wings and adjusted its stance within its nest. The nest also hosted its fledgling and a host of other birds were circling in the sky. The vulture gazed upward and flew into space. I tell this to the lama of the Three Ages.

When I finished describing my dream, Marpa clapped his hands and instructed Dakmema to prepare a feast. Turning to me he smiled and said, "This is a dream full of good omens." Turning to address the others he declared, "What a marvelous dream Mila Vajra has shared with us! Here is my interpretation….."

The northern land of the world is Tibet, where the doctrine of the Buddha will spread.

The snow-clad mountain is the translator Marpa and the Kagyu teaching. The summit of snow which touched the sky is matchless insight without equal.

The light of the sun and moon turning around its peak, is meditation radiating wisdom and compassion throughout the cosmos.

The light dispelling darkness is compassion dispelling ignorance. The base of the mountain covering the whole earth is the pervasiveness of the teachings.

The four rivers flowing in the four directions, are the four basic aspects of instruction. The rivers quenching the thirst of all beings, signify the liberation of seekers everywhere.

All the rivers flowing in to the sea, show the eventual merging of novices' awareness with their masters' awareness. The many flowers which sparkled, represent pure enjoyment.

The great pillars rising in each of the first three directions are you seated here today, my most attained students, and how you will aspire to be great lamas in those regions. Each has the particular nature of the animal which rests upon the pillar.

The fourth pillar, the one that arose in the north, foretells the future achievements of Milarepa himself and indicates that he has the nature of a vulture.

Its out-spread wings indicate realization of the secret instructions. Its perch in the cliff shows that his life will be harder than the rock. The fledgling in the nest indicates that he will be inimitable.

The host of small birds circling nearby shows the widespread transcendence of the Kagyu doctrine. Gazing upwards indicates freedom from birth and death. Its flight in to space shows attainment of enlightenment.

"The work of this old man is winding down. The hour for you, my dearest students, to go out and share the doctrine is close at hand. This wonderful dream of Mila's has shown that our blessed teaching will spread throughout the four directions. Knowing that will come to pass pleases me greatly."

The following day, Marpa imparted the secret instruction of the Fire of Tummo, comparable to the glowing coals of a wood fire in the midst of chilly weather. As a gift, he gave me the hat of Maitrepa and some sacred cloth from Naropa. He then told me I was destined to wander in the barren mountains and in the snows, and through meditation, I would develop profound spiritual vision. But for the near term, he felt there was additional instruction and special initiations needed, and he preferred I stay nearby in order to shore up inner experiences in his presence. I then went in to seclusion at a different place which was a primitive room built in to a rock cavity. I sealed the heavy door shut and left a small opening. Marpa and his wife tended to my well being, including bringing a portion of every ritual feast. This they did with great tenderness.

During that time of seclusion, I would usually meditate for long periods, and did not normally fall asleep. But one morning I dozed off and had a vivid dream. In the dream I returned to my childhood village. My natural father's house was cracked like the frayed ears of an old donkey. Rain had leaked in and had ruined the sacred books of his library.

The adjoining field was over-run with weeds and my mother had died. My sister had left and become a wanderer, begging for provisions. I called to my mother and sister by name and when I awoke, my pillow was soaked in tears. I realized I did not know whether my mother was dead or alive. I became sorely homesick and compelled to return to my village to see how true was my dream. I unblocked the heavy door and went down the hill to see the lama. He was asleep. I bowed humbly at the head of his bed and whispered my concern to him.

At the moment the lama awoke, the sun shone through his window and its rays fell on his head. At the same time, his wife entered, bringing his morning meal. Upon seeing me, his first words were, "My son, why have you so suddenly broken your seclusion? It might create inner obstacles, and open the way for Mara and dark influences. Go back and resume your solitary retreat."

I told him of my dream, and how it created such doubts about the well being of my mother and sister—and how I yearned to find out what had transpired in the many years I had been absent; whether Zessay, my childhood betrothed, had married someone else, and to see whether my aunt and uncle were dead or alive. I also longed to see whether the house and field of my youth had fallen in to disrepair—but most of all I was concerned for my sister and mother. I promised Marpa I would return soon.

Marpa replied, "My dear son, when you arrived here, you said you were no longer attached to worldly things. You have been away from your village for several years. You may go if you want to, but by so doing, I doubt that we will meet again. The fact that you came to tell me, and found me asleep, foretells that we shall not see each other again in this life.

"Even so, the sun rising in space at this moment foretells that you will make the Buddha's teaching shine as splendidly as the sun. And the sun's rays falling on my head as I awoke, foretells that our Kagyu teaching will spread far and wide. The arrival of my wife bringing a meal at that moment signifies that, even if you don't have physical food at hand, you will be nourished by spiritual food."

Knowing that I would be leaving soon, the lama bestowed upon me the most secret teachings of the type that are only transmitted from master to chief disciple. The oral instructions included initiation to the Path of Awakening, and also complete instruction concerning the path to Enlightenment. He told me that the same instructions had been conveyed to him by Naropa and that they should, in turn, be transferred to my most prominent disciple when the time arises in the future. These are oral instructions and should not be written down, neither should they ever be traded for food or riches

or to please others—or that will incur the wrath of the dakinis. He went on to say that my lack of gifts to him in no way
diminished the transference of correct and complete instructions. Indeed, my alacrity and zeal for religion were more
than enough compensation, and brought him great joy.

Then he placed his hands on my head and said, "Son,
your departure is sad, but impermanence is the nature of all
things in the world. Before you depart, stay for a few days
and ponder upon the wealth of instruction you have received. If you have uncertainties about the dharma, perhaps
we can clarify them." Thus spoke lama Marpa.

And so I stayed several days and we engaged in conversa-
tions to clarify various aspects of the instructions. Dakmema
prepared a special feast. Afterwards, the lama asked whether
I believed in the tangible effects of spiritual transformation,
and I answered in the affirmative. He then said, "Take refuge
in the solitude of the barren mountains, the snows and the
forests. Devote yourself to meditation and reject the bonds of
passion that so strongly affect pleasure-seeking people—and
which bind them to endless cycles of emotional peaks and
valleys." He then mentioned several specific locations that
were well-suited for meditation and seclusion, and told me
to radiate spiritual energy far and wide from each place.

Then, as his eyes welled with tears, he continued, "We,
father and son, will not see each other again in this life. I will
not forget you and neither will you forget me. So, rejoice that
in the beyond, we will meet in the realm of the dakinis. One
day, it may come to pass that you will encounter an obstacle.
When that time comes, look at this note." The lama then
handed me a small scroll of paper sealed with wax.

At that point, Dakmema wept. Her husband said, "Dear wife, why shed tears? Because Mila Vajra Banner-of-Victory has obtained the oral tradition from his lama and is about to go to meditate in the barren mountains? Is that a reason for tears? A more justified cause for tears, is the thought that millions of sentient beings are not aware of their potential to become Buddhas. Those beings will therefore live in confusion and die in misery. Millions are blessed with being born as humans, and furthermore, they hear of the dharma but, yet, don't take advantage of their potential to attain spiritual enlightenment—that is a true cause for tears."

Dakmema replied, "Yes, that is true, but I am not weeping now for universal concepts. I am sad because our spiritual son, who is so full of faith, fervor, wisdom and devotion, is leaving us tomorrow, and we may never meet again in this life."

That next morning, a group of us set off. Accompanying me were the lama, his wife and several fellow monks. After a half-day's journey, we reached a ridge with a magnificent view of the mighty Himalayan peaks to the south and the vast Tsampo valley along the north. We stopped to prepare and eat a simple meal, and sang salutations of departure to each other. All those present wept. I parted from the group walking backwards, reluctant to leave, yet knowing it was my karmic destiny to do so. I wondered again whether I would ever return. I walked until the others were just dark spots on the next ridge. I gave a last wave of my arm, then turned and headed first to visit Lama Ngokpa. I did this so we could compare our knowledge of the teachings. We found that in explaining the Tantra, he surpassed me—but in summoning the dakinis and their instructions, I surpassed him. After paying respects, I went on to my home village. A trek of that distance would ordinarily take ten days, but I was able to complete it in three without fatigue—which was a testament to my physical shape and spiritual development.

Thus ends Chapter Five.

Chapter 6

As I neared the village of my childhood, I encountered some shepherds. I pointed to the property that was willed to me and, feigning ignorance, I asked the shepherds what they could tell me about it. They replied that years ago, that field had belonged to a prosperous man who had developed it, and built a large house called Four Columns and Eight Beams.

I asked why there was now no house to be seen, and they replied, "When the father died, he read out his will, that his young son should inherit the property when the boy became of age. Because his relatives were greedy, the boy and his family received nothing. When the boy grew up, he became a mean magician and punished the people of the village by casting spells and sending hailstorms."

It was clear that the shepherds did not recognize who I was, so I asked them why the property had fallen in to such disrepair. They replied that the remaining villagers were superstitious and were afraid to go near it, particularly because there was a rumor the boy's mother had died in there, and her corpse was haunting the place.

I asked about the son and daughter, and they said, "The boy's little sister has grown and disappeared; perhaps she's become a beggar. As for the son, no one knows where he is, or whether he is dead or lost. If you dare, go down to the property and see it for yourself."

This news that my mother had died and my sister was a wandering tramp, filled me with sorrow. I lay low until the sun went down, then I warily went over to the property. I entered by moonlight and saw the ruined remains of the once proud house of my father. Gaps in the roof had let in rain, and cherished books in the library were soiled by dirt and rat droppings. I entered the main room, and there at the hearth was a pile of bones. In a heart wrenching moment, I realized those were the remains of my mother, who must have sat there in her last dying moments.

A wave of emotion and grief flowed over me, but just as suddenly I remembered lama Marpa's counsel to not get entangled in worldly emotions. Unifying my consciousness with my mother, and the enlightened consciousness of the Kagyu lamas, I gently sat upon my mother's bones, and meditated upon the transitory nature of all worldly things. I focused on pure awareness and was not distracted for a moment by body, speech or meanderings of the mind. Through intense meditation, I visualized the liberation of my mother and my father from suffering, and the unending cycle of life and death. After meditating for seven days and nights, I emerged with a plan to go to a cave at Horse Tooth White Rock. I made a vow to meditate there, in strict seclusion, for the rest of my life and further pledged that I would kill myself if I succumbed to dwell upon the worldly desires, or pleasures of the flesh, or lust for fame or fortune.

I gathered up and cleansed the bones of my mother, and arranged with a devout villager for them to be housed in a chorten. I cleaned the books from the library, and offered them to the villager as payment for the task. Together, he and I respectfully ground the bones to a powder, then mixed it with water. We then formed the clay in to figurines representing my little family and a few deities. We then placed them in a central cavity of a chorten.

The villager was the trusted son of the tutor who taught me to read when I was a boy. As we were making the figurines, he asked me several questions. He already knew much of the story of my hardships growing up, and the subsequent black magic that I had brought upon the village. He suggested, now that I was a man, I could marry Zessay and start a family. Quite sensibly, he went on to suggest I could reclaim my property, re-build the house and establish myself as a pillar of the community. Then he asked what I had been doing the past several years, during which no one had heard anything about me.

I explained I had been studying religion with a great teacher named lama Marpa. The villager had heard of the venerable Marpa, and that bolstered his argument, "Topa-ga, you can follow in the footsteps of lama Marpa and establish a monastery here. You would have a loving wife, a house, the teachings, and all that's needed."

I replied, "My friend, son of my now deceased tutor, you need to understand, lama Marpa took a wife and established a monastery for the benefit of sentient beings, and that's excellent, but that's not my dharma. To try to follow his lead, would be like a hare thinking it could follow in the footsteps of a snow leopard. My path is to meditate in solitude.

"It is not just my choice, but it was the express recommendation of lama Marpa. I returned to this village chiefly to find out about my mother and sister, and to check the status of the property. What I found, has only intensified my wish to meditate—like a flame burning in my breast. I plan to dedicate myself to meditating—without regard for food, clothing, fame or family. Indeed those things distract my focus. Solitary meditation in seclusion is most important in my quest toward spiritual enlightenment."

The next day, as I was about to leave, my tutor's son kindly gave me some provisions—consisting of a sack of barley and some dried meat. I knew of a good cave not far from my village, so I went in to seclusion there. I was able to meditate deeply for several months, but my body weakened from having to stretch the provisions so thin. I was compelled to go to the village to beg for food.

Walking with my staff, I came across a common tent, and called out, asking for food. Much to my surprise, it happened to be my aunt's tent. She came out, and as soon as she recognized me, she became furious and set her dogs on me. I held the dogs at bay as best I could, with stones and my staff. My aunt grabbed a tent pole and came at me shouting, "Disgraceful son of a noble father! Destroyer-demon of your own village! We thought you were dead; why do you come here? Be gone!"

She beat me to the ground, and even as my face was in a puddle of dirty water, she continued to flail at me with the tent pole. With all my effort, I scrambled free and traveled on, but news of my presence was spreading through the village.

A man appeared forty paces in front of me with a large stone in his hand. He called out in my direction, "You bastard!" I recognized the voice, as that of my uncle. He continued, "You are a disgrace to your father's memory. Is it not enough that you've brought ruin to your village?" He then threw the stone, narrowly missing my head. Other villagers gathered, and my uncle was compelling them to attack me.

Realizing my dire situation, which was compounded by my weakened state from barely eating for months, I had to think fast. I called out skyward, "Oh masters of black magic, oh ocean of guardian deities, drinkers of human blood, this dharma-practicing monk is surrounded by enemies, who threaten to do me harm. Come protect me! Though I may die this night, my guardian deities are ageless and will avenge my death."

Sobered by my incantation, the villagers restrained my uncle and he gradually stopped shouting at me. Those with stones in their hands, dropped them. One by one, others came forward and made humble offerings. I thanked them and left. That evening I had a vision foretelling a nice encounter if I stayed, so I found a quiet spot at the outskirts of the village.

The girl I was supposed to marry, Zessay, found me and we talked for a while. She brought some beer and some provisions. She confirmed that my mother had died, and my sister had become a wanderer. Much of the sadness I had felt early on resurfaced, and she comforted me. I asked her why, in all these years she had not married. She replied that other young men were afraid of my guardian deity. She was somewhat, but not very surprised that I had chosen a life of a renunciate monk, and asked what plans I had with my property which had fallen in to disrepair. I told her that if my sister Peta returned, she can inherit it. In the meantime, Zessay can use the field to grow crops.

She asked whether I might want to develop the property as a religious compound. I told her that I am not a religious man in the common sense, of donning red and yellow robes of fine cloth, and developing a temple and filling it with valuable religious texts.

She said she had never seen a religious man look as disheveled as me, with tattered clothes hanging on a thin frame. "You look worse than a beggar. What kind of Mahayana Buddhism is this?"

I told her it is the purest type of Mahayana, and how it renounces worldly desires in order to realize enlightenment. I asked her to renounce worldly things and follow the same path, but she said she could study the dharma in her own fashion. She made it clear, she would never dress in rags and starve herself in the name of religion. With that, she said goodbye and left.

My aunt got word that I had no use for my property, and that I was determined to go to caves and meditate. She hatched a plan that might allow her to gain possession. After a couple of days, she came to me bearing ample supplies of barley flour, beer and some dried meat, and said, "I apologize for siccing my dogs on you, and for beating you with a tent pole. It appears you have embraced the life of a holy hermit, and if so, you will forgive me. I have decided, since you don't want to be involved with your field, I will cultivate it and, in exchange, I will bring you provisions." Thus spoke my aunt.

I knew she was cunning, but even so, I agreed that if she could bring me a sack of barley every month, she could go ahead and cultivate my field, and keep the remainder of the harvest. I returned to a secluded cave and meditated.

As the ensuing months passed by, she only brought the agreed-upon sacks of barley for the first two months. Then two months passed with no provisions. She then came to visit, and was concerned that others were gossiping, saying that my field was haunted and that I might some day cast evil spells again, if things don't go my way. I told her that those days were over, and that no one need be worried about black magic coming from me. She tended to believe me, but wanted me to back it up with a sworn oath. I suspected that she wanted the oath because she was thinking of reneging on our agreement.

Though I made renewed efforts to meditate, at that time I was unable to experience profound insights—not even the experience of inner warmth by way of the Fire of Tummo. A while later, during which no provisions were brought, I had a vivid dream. I was plowing a strip of ground at my field. The earth was particularly hard, and I wondered whether I should give up. Then the venerable Marpa appeared in the sky and said, "My son, strengthen your will, have courage, you will be able to plow that strip of hard dry earth." I kept plowing and, with Marpa's encouragement, it worked and right away a thick and abundant harvest sprung up.

I awoke full of joy, and thought, "Since dreams are nothing more than projections of hidden thoughts, not even fools believe they are real. I should know better than to bank on dreams." Even so, I took this dream to mean that if I persevere in my efforts to meditate deeply, I would attain higher levels of inner experience. From that juncture, I resolved to go meditate at the cave at Horse Tooth White Rock.

As I was getting ready to depart, my aunt showed up carrying a sack. She said, "Here, take these provisions as payment for your field. You say you have no use for it. The villagers are vengefully angry at you, and because of my involvement with your property, they swear vengeance against me also. That is why it is best for you to take this payment and be gone. Go away and don't come back, otherwise the villagers might kill you, and kill me too for my association with you."

I knew my aunt was lying and that it was just a ruse to gain possession of my field. I also knew some of the villagers feared retribution from my threats of black magic. I could still send hailstorms, but privately, I did not want to do that any more. Anger and revenge were not now part of my consciousness.

I then realized that it was largely due to my aunt and uncle that I became drawn to the path of religion. Without the sufferings brought upon me and my family by their actions, I would not be well on the way to attaining spiritual liberation. I realized that holding on to possessions such as the property, would be like a lodestone around my neck. Far better that I cut the bonds of attachment and move toward my true goal. While my aunt was seated there on a rock, I sang these words to her:

> Defilement bursts the vital energy of liberation. People cultivate evil deeds. By indulging in such deeds, they suffer the miseries of the lower realms.

> If one hoards food and wealth and property, it becomes the envy of others.

> Everything one can accumulate eventually becomes the property of one's enemies. Tea and beer when craved are poisons. If I drink them, I will burst the artery of liberation.

The price you paid for my property is your cunning and
   avarice.

For me to retain even part of it, would be like being reborn
   among hungry ghosts.

Aunt, take my house and field. Take them, and may it
   bring you contentment. Oh gracious lama Marpa, im-
   mutable in essence, bless this monk that he may fulfill
   his destiny in the solitude of the mountains.

After a pregnant silence, my aunt exclaimed, "Nephew,
you truly are a sincere seeker. What you've decided is marvelous!" With a spring in her step, she departed.

I inspected the provisions, and was glad to see three bags
of barley, some dried meat and some butter. She had also
brought a worn-out fur coat and a thin cloak of white linen.
I sat and felt a mix of emotions. I was used to long periods
of solitude, so even simple interactions with people could be
rather intense. On the one hand, I was relieved to be done
with being a property owner. I felt it was time to move on to
a more secluded place, where I could meditate in earnest—
without interruptions, and I now had provisions to do so. I
named this cave near my village, Cave of the Foundation.

I hiked the entire next day and arrived late afternoon at
Horse Tooth White Rock without anyone knowing. I found
a suitable alcove, made a small hard mat for a cushion, and
then made a vow not to leave to descend to an inhabited
place, so long as I have not attained the full state of spiritual
enlightenment. I further vowed not to seek medicine if I get
sick, nor to seek clothing if I get cold, nor to beg for food,
even if I faced starvation. Altogether, I would strive, with the
blessings of my lama, the dakinis, and the guardian deities,

to become a living Buddha—or die trying. Then I sang this song,

> Oh my lama, son of Lord Naropa, bless this monk so that he may achieve the path to liberation. Shelter me from the distracting forces of Mara, and increase the depth of my meditation.
>
> Without attachments to the lake-bed of inner tranquility, may the lotus of transcendent insight bloom within me.
>
> Let no doubts inhabit my consciousness, but may the fruit of awakening grow ripe.
>
> Let not the Maras create obstacles. May an absolute focus arise in my mind.
>
> On the path to enlightenment, may the son follow in the adept manner of the father.
>
> Oh ever-compassionate lama, bless this monk, that he may attain perfection in the solitude of the mountains.

Having said that prayer, I sat in meditation day and night. Once a day I would make a thin soup with a bit of roasted barley flour. As the days passed, an awareness arose in my mind concerning the great spiritual symbol called Mahamudra. However, I could not sufficiently control my breath, because my body was weakening. Winter had started, and I was cold. I tried, but could not generate the spiritual bliss of the Fire of Tummo.

In quiet desperation, I invoked lama Marpa. One night, while in a state of inner realization, a group of beautiful dakinis surrounded me and said, "Marpa has sent us to tell you, that if you cannot generate the Fire of Tummo, you may use these yogic methods as a tune-up for your body."

They demonstrated yogic asana postures. Earlier I had thought that body postures focused too much on the physical, and might take away from the mental focus of meditation. But I came to realize that yoga postures and meditation were harmonious with each other. I realized physical satisfaction, through the sitting position known as the six interwoven hearths. I found vocal energy, through tantric channeling of breath. My mental strength increased, through a practice called The Self-Releasing Snake's Coil. After a while, I was glad to feel the Fire of Tummo spreading through my body, most notably, my chest and back.

After a year of seclusion, I was tempted to leave the cave and refresh myself and replenish my provisions. I prepared to leave, but then recalled my vow of a year earlier. So instead, I sang this song of affirmations:

> Oh Marpa, upholder of infinite truth, bless this monk, that
>   he may complete his retreat in solitude.
>
> I am cut off from friends and their pleasant talk.
>
> Cut off, too, am I from the views of the magnificent
>   valley.
>
> Cut off am I from all external things that can lift my
>   heart.
>
> I will not indulge in wandering thoughts, therefore my
>   mind will be tranquil. If I indulge in distractions, I will
>   succumb to unwholesome thoughts.

I will stay attentive, otherwise devotion will be carried away, as if by the wind.

I will not leave, but instead will stay where I am.

If I leave, I will stumble. I will not seek pleasure, but instead strive for control of mind.

Seeking pleasure will serve no purpose in my pursuits.

I will not sleep, but instead meditate.

If I sleep soundly, the five poisons of corruption might creep in to my consciousness.

Stylized depiction of Milarepa taken from a thanka painting

Having thus firmed my resolve, I placed a few more rocks in the spaces where the light shone in, and renewed my solitary meditation. One sack of barley, parsimoniously parceled out, was just barely enough to sustain me for a year. If I had ingested any less, I would surely have perished.

It got to where I did not distinguish night from day and the quality of my meditations improved. When a man finds a tiny bit of gold, he rejoices. If he loses it, he despairs. If he knew of the preciousness of spiritual enlightenment—he would know it to be more precious than a mountain of gold. Losing the chance to attain enlightenment in this lifetime, would be a better reason for him to despair. Though this quest be noble, it would be for naught, if my body were to die. After three years in the solitude of the cave, and having depleted my store of provisions, I was compelled to search for some new form of nourishment.

Thus ends Chapter Six.

Chapter 7

I WENT OUT OF THE CAVE OPENING, and basked in the lovely warmth of the sun. I drank sparkling water from a nearby tumbling rivulet. Stinging nettles grew in profusion nearby, and I found that by scalding them in water, they provided a nutritious, though rather monotonous food. When weather permitted, I meditated under the shade of a large rhododendron bush, and indulged in the expansive view of the valley.

My clothes were tattered. Months passed, and I ate only scalded nettles. I became like a skeleton with greenish-white skin stretched across its bones. I could push fingers in my stomach, and feel the lower part of my spine. The head on my hair became matted, and my body hair became grayish. I still had the tiny waxed scroll from my lama, and at times I thought of opening it. Instead, I placed it on my head during meditation. It helped allay feelings of hunger. Yet another year passed.

One day some hunters, who had no luck hunting lower down, chanced upon my cave. Upon seeing me, they shouted, "Ack, it's a ghost!" and cowered away. I called out that I was a man. They returned, peering at me like kids. When convinced I was a man and not a ghost, one said gruffly, "We're hungry. Where is your food?" I told them I had none except nettles.

They threatened me, but soon realized it was doing no good. Then they waxed playful and wondered how lightweight I was. One by one, they picked me up in my lotus sitting position and dropped me straight down. It caused me pain, but I did not harbor anger toward them.

Another year passed by. My clothes were seriously worn out, and the old fur coat given to me by my aunt was in tatters. The bits of fur were used to shore up the meditation cushion and, at night, I would pull pieces up to cover parts of my lower body from the cold. The shirt I had earlier had disintegrated from age. The only bit of material I had for my upper body, were pieces from the cotton cloth barley sacks. I thought to sew them in to some semblance of a garment, but I had neither needle nor thread. Instead, I knotted the ends of the three pieces of cloth, to make a makeshift cover for parts of my thin frame. In spite of my mastery of the Fire of Tummo, there were still periods of extreme cold, where I barely survived. In this way, another year of meditation passed.

Voices of many men were heard approaching. Some hunters, laden with game, arrived at the entrance to my cave. Seeing me, the closest one cried, "Ghost!" and ran away. His comrades doubted there could be ghosts in the daytime, and ventured in to get a better look. Timidly, the men approached me. I told them matter-of-factly that I was not a ghost but rather a monk meditating in seclusion. They asked why I had become so thin with a greenish hue to my skin. I explained that I had been eating nothing but nettles for a long time. They graciously offered me a good supply of meat along with other provisions. The leader said, "What you are doing is truly wondrous. Please enable the creatures we have killed to be reborn as humans. As for us, please pray for our sins to be washed away." With that, they said goodbye and left.

I was very pleased at my good fortune. Now I could eat like a human being. As I started eating cooked meat, my health improved and my senses became keener. I experienced prolonged states of blissful emptiness. I portioned the meat sparingly but by doing so, enabled maggots to infest the remnants. I thought to pick them out, but then decided that maggots have a right to nourishment also, so I let them have the remaining bits of meat. Soon, I returned to my diet of nettles.

One late afternoon, a solitary man showed up and, without greeting me or identifying himself, rummaged throughout the entire cave—looking for some bit of food. I burst out laughing for the first time in years and said, "Just try finding something to eat in the low light of evening, when I can find nothing even in the light of day." He also laughed, and then departed.

Another year passed, and my physical body barely survived, though my mental insights soared like the wings of an eagle.

One day after a rain, some hunters came along the trail to the entrance of my cave. They had not been able to shoot any game that day. One of them chanced to look in the cave, and saw me in a deep meditative state, and gasped, "Is it a man or a ghost, or maybe it's a scarecrow that someone placed in here as a jest?"

I smiled and told him it is just a man.

He was a hunter from my home village and, from the gap in my front teeth, recognized me, "Are you Topa-ga?"

I responded in the affirmative.

"We have been searching for game all day and haven't found any. Give us something to eat, and we will pay you back later. Topa-ga, you left our village years ago. Have you been holed up here all this time?"

I told him I had, and that I didn't have anything they would want to eat. He asked what I normally eat, and I told him I ate scalded stinging nettles, and offered him the same. He and his friends chuckled about that, while helping make a fire, and we sat around eating the cooked weeds. One hunter said it was an unpleasant taste, and asked for meat. I told him, if I had meat, then my food would be nourishing and I wouldn't look like a bag of bones. He then went on to ask for bones or salt. I told him that if I had bones or salt, I could then make a broth, and the nettles would not be so tasteless.

Another in the group said frankly, "Topa-ga, with the way you're starving yourself and your tattered clothing, you will never look normal. You barely look human. Even the lowest servant eats better than you, and wears decent clothing. There must be no man on earth more miserable than you."

I asked him to not be so quick to judge my state of being. I then briefly recounted the story of my family's plight, and how I came to be in this state. I then went on to say, "I consciously chose this mode of living—as this is the most direct path for me to attain my true Buddha nature. There is no worldly man braver, nor anyone with higher aspirations than I. Although you were fortunate enough to be born in a land with access to the Buddha's teaching, you do not even strive for the dharma, let alone meditate. Rather than being the most miserable man on earth, I could well be the most content—indeed I may be one of the most blissful men. Here, listen to this song called 'The Five-Fold Happiness.'"

I prostrate at the feet of Marpa the compassionate. Bless
my renunciation in this life. Horse Tooth White Rock
is the Fortress of the Middle Way. At the summit, this
cotton-clad Tibetan monk has renounced food and
clothing in this life to become a Buddha.

I am happy with the hard cushion beneath me. I am happy
with the cotton cloth which covers me. I am happy with
the meditation cord which ties my knees and enables
me to sit comfortably. I am happy with this ghost-like
body, neither starved nor sated. And I am happy with
my mind which has gained profound insight.

If it appears to you that I am happy, do as I have done.
If you do not have the good fortune to be religious,
consider the latent happiness of all beings, of you and
me, and do not take misguided pity on me.

Now the sun is setting, return to your homes. Since life is
short and death strikes without warning, I who strive
toward enlightenment have no time for idle words.
Therefore please leave me to my meditation.

The lead hunter said, "Topa-ga, you have said many
fascinating things here this afternoon. You certainly have
a gift for speech and for spontaneously creating songs. Yet,
however commendable your example, we cannot follow the
way you have embraced." With those words, they got up,
said goodbye sweetly, and departed.

Each year at my village, a large festival is held which
showcases the casting of figurines. Detailed molds are made
of copper or wood, into which a special clay is poured. The
clay is a mixture of pulverized bones of people and animals,
along with the ashes of people who have been cremated.
The hunters who had visited my cave were there and were
getting drunk and were singing "The Five-Fold Happiness,"

trying to recall the words as best they could in their merry stupor.

My sister Peta happened by, and remarked, "Whoever wrote those words is an enlightened being."

One of the hunters laughingly remarked, "Well look at little Peta, and how she praises her brother."

She said, "Why are you talking about my brother? He is long-departed."

The hunter responded, "He may be barely in existence, but he's not departed. In fact, we don't know whether he's a living Buddha, or whether he's the most miserable man, starving himself to death. But we did sit with him recently, and he sang us this song."

Peta retorted, "Don't tease me, you drunken mutts. My family has suffered so much already, and I am now abandoned with no one to turn to." And she turned away to weep privately.

Zessay heard the commotion and came up to Peta and put an arm around her shoulders. "Don't cry, sister. Your brother is indeed alive, or at least he was a few years ago when I saw him. He came through the village and made a pledge to be a renunciate. He was talking about going to meditate in seclusion, up at Horse Tooth White Rock. He may still be alive. If so, he would surely need provisions. Peta, why don't you go, and see if he's up there in that region."

Full of anticipation, Peta packed some provisions and headed out to Horse Tooth White Rock. It was a long, tiring trek. When she first cast eyes upon me, she was aghast, and like the others before, thought she was beholding a ghost. My body was wasted by asceticism to such a degree that my eyes had sunk in their sockets, every bone protruded, my skin was dried out with a greenish hue, and had a cracked wax-like covering. The hair on my head was a dizzying tangle of gray. I recognized my sister standing there, frozen in place, and I broke the silence by saying, "I am your brother, Mila Topa-ga."

She recognized my voice and came to embrace me. "Brother, my elder brother!" she cried, then collapsed in my arms while fainting.

I set her gently on a smooth rock, and after a few moments she revived. She took another wide-eyed look at me, then placed her head on my bony knees and, covering her face with her hands, sobbed while saying, "Our mother died of grief and longing for her only son, and no one came to even bury her. I had no suitors because other men thought I was from a cursed family, so I gave up all hope and left the village. I went to another province to beg. I didn't know if you were dead or, if you were alive, if you were still practicing black magic. Now I find you, and see you are starving. We must be the saddest brother and sister in the four directions. Oh father, Oh mother, who can see us from the world beyond, behold your children who are stuck in misery." Then Peta wept, while her body heaved with emotion.

I stroked her hair and sang this song:

Obeisance to the venerable lamas. Bless this monk, that he may fulfill his task.

Oh sister, sentient being of the world, all joys and pains are fleeting. But since you grieve in this way now, I am certain that, for you there exists a lasting happiness. For this reason, listen to this song of your elder brother.

To give thanks to all sentient beings who are my parents, I do religious work in this place. This cave is like a lair for beasts; at the sight of it, others would be roused to indignation.

My food is less than that of dogs and swine. At the sight of it, others would be moved to nausea. My body is like a skeleton; at the sight of it, even a savage enemy would weep.

My behavior appears to be that of a madman, and my sister blushes with shame. But my awareness is that of a Buddha. Upon beholding it, the deities rejoice.

Even though my rump has become calloused from sitting so long on this cold stone floor, I have persevered. My body, inside and out, has taken on the essence of a nettle; it will never lose its greenness.

In this solitary cave in the wilderness, I admit this monk has known much loneliness, but my heart will never separate from the enlightened lamas of the Three Ages.

By the power of meditation arising from my efforts, I will heighten my state of awareness. When spiritual insights are attained, happiness comes of itself.

I ask you, dear sister Peta, instead of viewing all this in frustration and sorrow, to instead strive with perseverance toward the Dharma.

Thus I sang.

Peta responded, "If this is true, then your words are astonishing, and barely believable. If it is true that you have attained such happiness, then why aren't many others practicing this type of Dharma? From your appearance, you look miserable."

She then showed me the beer and food, which we shared. I ate and drank as if feasting. During that evening's meditation, my mind became crystal clear due, in no small part, to the added nutrition. Late the next morning, Peta bade me farewell and left.

Afterwards, my body felt ill at ease. I attributed it to the complexity of my body trying to digest so much food which it wasn't accustomed to. My mind was also affected in such a way, as to fluctuate between positive and negative thought patterns. For several days, my meditations were not as fulfilling as usual.

About that time, Peta returned, this time accompanied by Zessay. The provisions they brought comprised meat, butter, tsampa and a large crock of beer. It must have been a chore to haul all those things up the long rocky trail to the cave entrance. It so happened that a few moments before they arrived, I had gone to fetch water. Thinking I was on my own, I had neglected to wear any clothes. As I was walking up the creek from one direction, they were walking up the path from another, so we all arrived on the landing at the same moment. Seeing my emaciated nudity caused the two women to blush, while feigning to look away.

With residual giggles, they offered me the food and poured me a cup of beer. As we sat there visiting, Peta made the comment, "From whatever angle one looks at my brother, one cannot call him a man." She went on to suggest that I go to a village to beg for alms, and start back to eating the food that humans eat. She offered to help me get some clothing together. Zessay chimed in, saying she, too, would assist with provisions and clothes.

I told them, "I do not know when I will die, so any time I spend begging for food is time spent away from meditation. I do not want to indulge in good food, handsome clothes, nor lively talk, and laughter with friends, if it might detract from my spiritual goals through meditation. Peta, you look at me and you call me miserable, but that is not the reality. Let me sing you a song called 'Fulfillment of my Aim.'

"I invoke the lama to bless this monk so that he may complete his retreat in solitude."

> Were my happiness not known to relatives,
>> Were my misery not known to enemies,
>> Were I to die in solitude, the aim of this monk would
>> be fulfilled.

> Were my growing old not known to friends,
>> Were a dire sickness not known to my sister,
>> Were I to die in solitude, the aim of this monk would
>> be fulfilled.

> Were I to die unknown to men,
>> If my rotting corpse was unseen by vultures,
>> Were I to die in solitude, the aim of this monk would
>> be fulfilled.

> Were there no vigil around my corpse,
>> Were there no lamentations over my death,

> Were I to die in solitude, the aim of this monk would be
> fulfilled.

With no one to ask where I had gone,
>With no one to say where I was,
>Were I to die in solitude, the aim of this monk would
>be fulfilled.

In this remote cave in the mountains,
>May my wish be fulfilled for the benefit of all beings.

Thus I sang.

Zessay spoke up to say she was impressed with my depth of renunciation. However, my sister was not impressed, and continued to chide me for lack of proper food and clothing. She figured that, if I were determined to not beg for alms as she had been doing, then at least I could get hold of some

This portrayal of Milarepa shows him in the listening mudra (pose) with hand cocked behind his ear.

clothing that was less ridiculous than tying together spent barley sacks. To that end, she pledged to bring me something decent to wear.

After they left that day, I ate the rich food that they had brought. The resulting ups and downs of alternating pleasure and pain distressed me. It became clear that the Spartan diet I had become accustomed to, though it nearly caused me to starve to death, had nevertheless enabled me to meditate on an even keel. In contrast, the exotic tastes and variety of the lush food the women had brought, was causing pronounced fluctuations in my mental and physical state.

My distress was such that, for the first time in my many years of seclusion, I chose to break the seal of the scroll given to me by Lama Marpa. I then read it. The words he had written gave instructions for overcoming obstacles and for improving meditation practice. It went on to offer instructions for transforming vice in to virtue and, as if foreseeing my immediate dilemma, it advised that, now, it was all right to eat good food in moderation.

Thus ends Chapter Seven.

Chapter 8

M Y MEDITATIONS WENT TO A HIGHER LEVEL after that. It appeared as though, during all those many moons of meditating with minimal nourishment, my nerves had absorbed immense creative energy. The rich food and beer brought by Peta and Zessay had enabled that creative energy to be released—thereby affording sustained experiences of lucid bliss and pure awareness. I experienced the inherent simplicity of the Dharmakaya.

Imperfections effortlessly transformed into perfections. I realized that samsara, or negative thoughts and positive thoughts stem from the same source consciousness. In other words, all thoughts stem from a luminous state of emptiness.

Samsara is the result of channeling thoughts in a negative direction. Enlightenment results from realizing that empty source as perfect awareness. This state of bliss was the fruit of my previous meditations coupled with the transference of instructions by my lama. It was given impetus by the nutritious meals brought by Peta and Zessay.

I recalled the story of Gautuma Buddha, and how he first experienced blissful rapture while meditating under the Bo Tree in northern India. He too had been on a near starvation diet for many years—thinking, along with his fellow seekers, that extreme renunciation was the sole path to enlightenment. Then came the day when he departed from his fellows, and happened to wander to a park and sat beneath a large tree. That evening, a gopi milk-maid noticed him, and sensed something very special was about to take place. She pointed out the young man to her matron, and it was decided the gopi should bring a bowl of cooked rice in cream over to offer to the thin young man, who was sitting there. That simple bowl of food was the first real meal Gautuma had eaten after many months of fasting. The legacy of his meditation that night is legendary, and has inspired countless meditators since then.

With renewed vigor, my meditations encompassed wider dimensions. Often during the day, I felt as though I were levitating through the space within the cave, and flying around the surrounding environment outside. When night came, I felt I could explore the celestial universe. I would transform myself in to any number of material and spiritual beings, and would go visit many realms of the Buddhas and even attend their teachings. Sometimes I would be the teacher, spreading dharma with ease. My body could transform to flames or to spouting blessed water. There were times when I would be sitting within the center of a wonderfully large mandala—at times angular, other times circular. Buddhas, dakinis, saints, and other deities would be situated in surrounding sections, and we would commune together. The mandala became a multi-faceted projection of my enlightened mind—and brought intense and sustained bliss.

I was able to fly through space, so I flew to the Cave of the Eagle's Shadow and meditated there. It was there that a particularly intense Fire of Tummo arose within me, radiating blissful warmth. As I flew to return to Horse Tooth White

Rock, I passed over a small village in a valley, where a man was plowing with his son. The man used to live in the village of my childhood, and happened to have a grudge against me and my mother, stemming from the black magic spells from years ago. The son was leading the team of oxen as the father guided the plow. The son saw me flying high overhead, pointed and called out in glee. The father stopped, looked up and said, "It is that son of that wicked woman White Garland. He is a cunning practitioner of black magic, wracked by starvation. Son, don't let his shadow fall on you!"

The son retorted, "If that be a man, and he can fly—surely there is no greater spectacle than that!" and he went on looking at me until I passed beyond the hill.

I started to think that the time was right to work for the good of sentient beings. Then a prophecy of the yidam came to me. It advised that I devote myself to meditation, in accordance with the lama's instructions. I could fathom how a solitary life, devoted to spiritual meditation, could benefit all beings—though I felt that human interaction would play a part in my dharma later on.

I then decided that I had stayed at Horse Tooth White Rock long enough—and that it was time to move on. People were becoming aware of my presence here. As more time goes by, more people will come to visit and this will disturb my seclusion. Flying around certainly doesn't help to maintain a low profile.

I picked up the cooking pot used to cook nettles, and left the cave entrance. During long periods of meditation, one of my feet had become cramped. As I stepped out on the uneven ground, I stumbled and almost fell. The cooking pot fell loose, and rolled a little ways and broke. The residue from countless meals of nettles, had broken free and kept the bowl shape of the inside of the pot. I marveled at this, and felt inspired to sit down and sing the following brief poem:

> At the same moment I had a pot and I did not have a pot.
> This is an example of the impermanence of all things.
> In particular, it represents the human condition.
> If this is so, I Milarepa, will strive to meditate without distraction.
> This humble pot which aided my sustenance
> becomes my teacher at the very moment it breaks.
> This lesson on the inherent impermanence of all things is
> a marvel.

Thus I sang.

At that moment, several hunters happened by to take a mid-day break. The leader called out, "Oh hermit, we heard your melodious song through the bushes." When he came in to view, he exclaimed, "My, my, how did you become so thin and green?" I told him it's a wonder I'm alive, considering I've had so little to sustain my body.

The hunters were in a cheery mood, so they invited me to join with them, and share food. During the meal, a young man said to me, "You look like a capable person. If, instead of this life of depravation, you had lived a worldly life, you might have become a rich man and be riding a handsome horse, and eating good food."

The elder member of the group told the boy to hush up, saying, "Pay no mind to the kid. He has a rivalry with his neighbors, and has designs for buying a particular white horse. He tells us that he dreams about riding at full gallop, while flailing a big sword to smite his enemies. He doesn't understand that there are those among us who choose to get away from the business of village life, and the conflicts it brings." Then turning to me, he continued, "You hermit, though you look sad, you do indeed have a pleasant singing voice. Sing us another song... one for our spiritual benefit."

I told them, though I may appear miserable from my outside appearance—in truth there is no one happier than I. To explain my innate happiness, I sang this song called "Galloping Horse of the Renunciate."

I prostrate myself at the feet of Marpa the Compassionate.

In the mountain hermitage which is my body, in the temple of my breast, at the summit of the triangle in my heart, the horse which is my mind flies like the wind.

If I try to rope in the horse, what sort of lasso will I use? To try to secure him, to what sort of stake will I tie him? If he is hungry, what fodder shall I give him? If he is thirsty, where shall I find him water? If he is cold, what sort of shelter shall I house him in?

If I rope the horse in, I will do so with the lasso of non-discrimination. If I secure him, it will be to the stake of deep meditation. When he is hungry, I will feed him with the lama's instructions. When thirsty, I will bring him to the stream of mindful focus. If he is cold, I will shelter him within the walls of emptiness.

For saddle and bit, I will use skillful means and wisdom. I will direct him with the reins of life-sustaining energy. The shadow of my whip will be non-duality. The child of awareness will ride him.

The horse's rider will be perseverance. For a headdress, he will don the enlightened attitude of Mahayana.

His coat of mail will be fashioned from listening and meditation. His shield will be the shield of patience. He will hold the lance of perfect seeing. At his side will be the sword of knowledge.

If the arrow of his consciousness strays on its trajectory, he will straighten it without anger. Its feathers are the Kagyu teachings. Its tip is the sharp point of insight. The bow of divine emptiness is notched with compassion.

Measuring the infinite range of non-duality, he will loose his arrows throughout the world. Those who he strikes are the faithful ones. That which is killed is the worldly self.

He will strike against lust; he will protect against delusion. If he gallops, it will be upon the plains of great bliss. If he perseveres, he will attain enlightenment. Cutting back, he smites the root of samsara. Going forward, he reaches the exalted plain of Nirvana. Astride such a horse, one attains the highest enlightenment.

My friends, can regular happiness compare to this? I choose this sort of bliss over worldly happiness.

Thus I sang to the hunters.

Afterwards, our group talked about religion for a while longer, then the hunters grabbed their gear and went on their way.

For the first time in years, I set out toward civilization. I walked down a long winding trail. At a village called Dingri, I sat by the side of the road and watched people going by. A group of pretty girls approached and, seeing my emaciated body, one commented, "Look. What misery! May I never be reborn as such a creature."

Another chimed in, "How pitiful. A sight like that depresses me." The other girls gave me disdaining glances.

I felt compassion for these beings who knew no better, so I stood up and addressed them, "Dear sisters and daughters, there is no real reason for you to look down upon me. You have wrapped your self-esteem around your ordinary lives. With such immature and confused perceptions, deceitful people are honored like deities. So too, hypocrites are prized like gold, and the faithful are rejected like stones on the road."

After I spoke, one girl recognized me as someone she had heard her father talk about respectfully. She turned to the other girls and recommended they apologize. I spoke personally with this girl, and she gave me seven little shells she had picked up by the side of the road. Seeing me in a different way, the girls bowed and asked for instruction.

In response, I sang them a song about forgiveness:

I invoke the compassionate Lama. I offer this sacred dharma in a song.

Above, in the celestial mansion of the Devas, conventional dharma is preferred, whereas true doctrine in ignored.

Below, in the palace of the serpent deities, worldliness is preferred, whereas profound teaching is ignored.

In the middle, in the realm of Man, false teachers are preferred, whereas authentic teachers are ignored.

In the four regions of U and Tsang, rote learning is preferred, whereas meditation is ignored.

In the dark days of Kali Yuga, wicked people are preferred,
whereas the good are ignored.

In the eyes of these beautiful girls, the handsome man is
preferred, whereas the bedraggled monk is ignored.

In the ears of these young girls, the gopi's song sounds
pleasant, whereas the song of dharma sounds unpleasant.

This is my response to your lovely gift of the seven shells.
This is the celebration of your forgiveness.

Thus I sang.

And so, amid a profusion of smiles, the girls departed.
Then I too left for the region of Drin. I had heard of some
secluded caves near there. I picked one called Castle of the
Sun, and sat to meditate there.

Some months passed and my meditation deepened like
a grand ocean of bliss. Every so often, people would show
up offering food and drink. Though I appreciated that, I saw
it as distractions which interrupted my seclusion. I recalled
lama Marpa's instruction which mentioned a more secluded
cave at Lachi, so I decided to head to that region.

I found out later that at that same time, my sister Peta
had gone to Horse Tooth White Rock. She brought cloth,
which she had woven from wool and goat hair collected
from begging—and was hoping that I would craft it into a
cloak. Not finding me there, she searched elsewhere, asking
everyone she met. During the course of her travels, she saw
a famous lama dressed in rich garments of brocaded silk. He
sat upon an ornate throne sheltered beneath a canopy, made

to look like a multiple-headed serpent. When his monks blew on their long ceremonial trumpets, the ends of which curved upward from the ground, a large crowd of townspeople would gather, and deluge him with valuable gifts.

Peta was reminded of how people ordinarily treat a lama. It was in sharp contrast to her brother's mode of religion— which saw him shunning the company of others. She felt ashamed by the cruel things others had said about him— how he continued to eat like a field mouse and appeared to be stuck in misery.

When Peta found me, I looked much the same as when we parted company. With an imploring voice, she said, "Brother, your religion is one of deprivation. You still have no clothes and nothing to eat. You should hear what other people say; it's embarrassing. Well, at least you can make a loincloth from this material I brought. Here take it."

She continued, "I just passed by a monastery and saw the lama there, and how everyone, monks and laymen, treated him with respect and brought him gifts. He chants and does rituals for everyone and satisfies their wishes. That's the real kind of religion. Why not go to that lama and see whether he will accept you in to his service. Even if you were the least of his monks, you would be happier than you are now. You know I am too poor to continue to bring provisions. If you keep up this lifestyle of depravation, walking around naked in the snowy mountains, you may die." While she was speaking, she wept, but when she ended her speech, sobs come forth in full.

I answered by saying, " I acknowledge that my nudity embarrasses you, but this is my natural state. Indeed we are all born nude, so it's not something to be ashamed of. You should be more ashamed of your protruding breasts, which you were not born with. As for my habit of meditating without ample food or clothing, it is not through lack of alms, but rather it is my choice. When I see people indulge in the blatant pleasures of worldly desires, I am disgusted. It is like watching a man gorge himself with food until he vomits it all up. When I see men lusting after, and then forcing themselves on young women, it is similarly disgusting—like seeing a conniving man forcing himself upon my sister or mother.

"It is not only my choice to be a renunciate, but it was recommended by lama Marpa who advised I renounce worldly attachments, including wealth and fame. If I chose to become a monk with the rich lama, it would be the easiest thing to do. Even if I chose to sit on a gilded throne like him, and receive valuable gifts and adoration, that too would be easy for me to attain. But I've chosen a higher path."

Thus ends Chapter Eight.

Chapter 9

"Peta, you too could renounce worldly things, and come with me to the snows of Lachi to meditate. I assure you the sun of happiness would shine on you, if you would embrace renunciation, and turn your back on the worldly passions. Listen to your brother's song":

Dear Peta, young maiden consumed by desires of a worldly existence,

First, picture a parasol with a pinnacle of shiny gold. Second, see how it's encircled by a fringe of Chinese silk. Third, see the frame adorned as beautifully as a peacock's tail. Fourth, notice its ornate handles made of red sandalwood. A fine parasol with these four features, your elder brother could obtain if he so wished. Such enticing things ensue from worldly desires, which your brother has renounced, because the sun of happiness has risen for him.

Abandon the Eight Worldly Attachments, oh sister.

Abandon them and let us go together to the snows of Lachi.

First, you see the brightly painted monastery, high above the village. Second, you hear the eloquent speeches of a bright lama. Third, delicious butter tea is served, fresh and warm from the stove. Fourth, behold the procession of young monks, eager to serve. Such

enticing things ensue from the worldly desires, which
your brother has no use for. Peta, let us go together to
the snows of Lachi.

First, observe the rites and rituals, divination and astrology.
Second, hear the priestess, skilled in hypocrisy. Third,
partake in ritual feasts rife with sensual gratification.
Fourth, hear sweet chanting to charm female devotees.
Such enticing things ensue from the worldly desires,
which your brother has no use for. My sister, let us go
together to the snows of Lachi.

First, behold the majestic castle with its soaring tower.
Second, observe intense cultivation of surrounding
fields. Third, amass provisions and treasure by de-
ceptive means. Fourth, servants hone their intrigue.
These things your brother could attain, if he so wished.
Such enticing things ensue from the worldly desires,
which your brother has no use for. Dear Peta, let us go
together to the snows of Lachi.

First, the arched neck of a great stallion,
   Second, the ornamental saddle, studded with jewels,
   Third, the warrior brilliant in his armor,
   Fourth, the passion to subdue the enemy to protect
   his brethren,
   Such dazzling things ensue from worldly desires,
   which your brother has renounced because the sun
   of happiness arises.

Oh sister, abandon worldly attachments, let them fall by
the wayside, and let us go together to the snows of
Lachi.

Thus I sang.

"Peta, if you cannot contemplate renouncing worldly attachments, and if you cannot fathom going with me to the

snows of Lachi, then your sisterly concerns distract me. All this talk of worldly things disturbs my meditation. From the moment of birth, one does not know when he will die. I don't have time to postpone these endeavors. I have made a pledge to meditate in seclusion according to the instructions of lama Marpa. That is why I am heading to a cave at Lachi."

Peta then replied, "Mila, what your high sounding words call 'worldly attachments,' ordinary people call; living life day to day. You and I, brother and sister, have gained no happiness, so we have no happiness to give up. I will not go to Lachi and deprive myself of food and clothing. I do not even know where Lachi is! And I like warmth too much to go someplace with snow all around. Rather than darting among the rocks like deer pursued by hounds, why not stay in one place? People in this region seem to respect you as some sort of holy hermit. Plus, if you stay in one place, it is easier for me to find you. Here, make yourself a cloak from this material, and I will return in a few days."

I agreed to stay put for a while. While she was away, I did my best to sew the material into something wearable, though I had no experience with needle and thread. Remembering the many cold times in caves, I made a hood to cover my head and sewed individual little sleeves for my fingers at the end of the arm pieces. At the bottom, I sewed pockets for my feet. Knowing that my exposed penis had been a topic of conversation, and had caused embarrassment for others, I made sure to fashion a sleeve for it too.

When Peta returned, she asked me to don the new cloak. When she saw it on me, she exclaimed, "Look at you! Look at what you've done! Not only are you without shame, but you have ruined the cloth which I wove with such care."

Bandying around the word "shame" inspired me to give an opinion on what that word meant:

"Peta, worldly people feel shame over things which are natural, like nudity—while unabashedly indulging in things which are truly shameful, such as evil deeds and hypocrisy. Worldly people partake in robbery, fraud and betrayal of friends—surely those things are truly worthy of being called 'shameful?'"

Peta responded with something that our mother used to say, "No matter what is said, he won't listen." Though I didn't request aid from her, she pledged to bring me provisions when she could. As she was about to leave, I asked her one more time to consider studying the Dharma.

I told her that, even if she did no real religious practices, she should stay nearby as long as the provisions held out. Reluctantly at first, she agreed. So we traveled together in the direction of Lachi. During those weeks, I explained as much as I could about the law of karma. Over time, I could see her gaining an appreciation for Dharma, and commensurately, her desire for worldly things decreased.

It so happened that not long before, my uncle had died. My aunt, feeling alone and sad, decided to look for me. She went from village to village, leading a dzo loaded with provisions. At each place, she would ask if anyone had seen an emaciated ghost-like person with wild hair. At Drin, some villagers directed her in the right direction. Having tethered the dzo in a safe place, she carried what she could and found her way to the cave where my sister and I were practicing dharma. Peta, standing on a rock ledge, was the first to see her. Much of Peta's pent-up anger from childhood came to the fore, and she was adamant about not allowing her aunt access to the cave. Peta pulled back a log which connected an outlying ledge with the cage entrance.

"Peta, do not pull back that log. Your aunt is here to see you and your brother."

Peta countered, "That's why I pulled it back."

"Yes, yes, I understand. You have reason to reject me. I was sometimes callous when you were in my care. But now things have changed. I have changed. I have a deep remorse for things that happened in your childhood. Really. Peta dear, I have come to find your brother, so put back the log bridge. If you can't do that, at least tell him I am here." Thus spoke my aunt.

I had heard the commotion from the other side of a rock outcrop, so I climbed to the ledge to observe the drama. My aunt saw me and prostrated herself repeatedly in my direction. I realized I would see her eventually, because not seeing someone who sincerely seeks an audience would be contrary to the dharma. But I felt compelled to first rebuke her, so I said, "As you may know, I have given up attachments to relatives, and in particular my aunt and uncle who have caused my family such grief.

"Oh aunt, do you remember what you have done? If you have forgotten, I will remind you with this song I will call 'The Demon Within.'"

> In the land of Kya-Ngatsa, we, mother and children lost
> our noble father. Then all our wealth was taken from
> us, and we were given misery in return.

We were pushed aside like moldy tsampa, by you and
your husband.

From that day on, I gave up all attachments to relatives.

But after years of wandering, I longed to see my mother
and sister, so I returned home. My mother was dead
and my sister gone. Under the weight of sadness, I
devoted myself wholly to meditation.

Still later, when I was hungry, I left my cave to beg, and
found myself at my aunt's tent.

Recognizing the depraved hermit, she was prompted to
anger and vengeance. She called her dog, and set
him upon me. Using a tent pole as a stick, she beat
my body as one flails a sheaf of grain. I fell face-down
in a pool of water. As I was about to lose my life, she
yelled, "monster of evil!" and reviled me as the shame
of my family.

My heart, crushed by these terrible words, was riven with
pain and roused to fury.

Breathless and stunned, I could not speak. Later, with
thinly disguised deception, my aunt took my property.
A demon lives in my aunt's body. From that day on, I
abandoned all feelings for her.

Further down the road, my uncle, with evil in his heart, cast
stones at me, nearly crushing my skull—which would
have taken away my life's breath. He cursed me with
every sort of vile word. At that moment, I was again
close to death. A callous butcher's heart beats within
my uncle's body. From that day on, I abandoned all
feelings for him.

To this renunciate, relatives are more cruel than enemies.
Later, when I sought shelter away from the village,

faithful Zessay, who could not forsake me, came to me
with tenderness.

> With affectionate words, she consoled my wounded heart.
> With nourishing food and drink she eased my hunger
> and thirst. I am deeply grateful to her. Even so, except
> for devotees of the dharma, I have no need to see
> anyone, and still less reason to see my aunt. So leave
> now while it is still day.

Thus I sang.

My aunt was reduced to tears, and repeatedly prostrated
fully prone with her head touching the cold stone, saying,
"Nephew, I now see that you are right. I feel terrible about
the pain I caused. My husband has recently died and now I
feel so alone. Please accept my deep-felt remorse. I still want
to stay. There is nowhere else I can go. If you do not let me
stay for at least a while, I will kill myself." Thus she spoke.

I was about to replace the log across the chasm, when Peta
grabbed my arm and took me aside—whispering additional
reasons why we should not accept our aunt in to our lives. I
told Peta that I felt bound by the dharma to receive her, so I
put the log back in place. My aunt was allowed to stay, and
I spoke to her at length about the law of karma. She camped
out nearby, and wound up focusing on the dharma. Months
later, she became a yogini, and achieved a degree of liberation
through meditation.

I was finally able to break away to travel to the snows of
Lachi. There, I resumed my focus on meditating in seclusion,
and firmed my belief that, if a person truly believes in the
emptiness of things, he would perceive the interdependence
of cause and effect, as being inherent in emptiness itself.

Apparently, word was spreading throughout the region about my renunciation and adherence to the dharma.

As the months stretched out, I would travel from one cave to another, and more often than not, a seeker would show up and request teachings. Some were young men, some were older than I, and a few were women. Some seekers would bubble over with praise and enthusiasm, while others were quietly contemplative. Some were eager to absorb every tidbit of teaching like a sponge, while others were critical to a fault—as impervious to the teachings as seasoned teakwood is to soaking up water.

One time, after I had just crossed a raging river on a shaky bamboo bridge, a young man approached from the other direction. He was dandily attired in a velvet dress shirt and was riding an imposing white horse. As I was relaxing by the side of the path, he didn't notice this thin man sitting there, until he and his steed were almost upon me. Startled, he called out, "Old tramp, you startled my horse and almost caused us to fall in to the steep gorge! You look as white as the rocks, why don't you get some real work."

I told him I didn't mind being mistaken for a rock, and asked him where he was going in such handsome attire. The boy said he was going to be a successful businessman in the big town, and that he would never fall so low as to be a beggar crumpled down by the side of a path.

I told him I was not a beggar and asked, in this song, if he thought the pursuit of business would bring him happiness:

> Young man so dandy and handsome, there is little doubt
>   your efforts will bring success in business. Though by

gaining success, others must suffer loss. Yet success in worldly ways is fraught with peaks and valleys. Better by far, to gain success of bodhichitta—where no one suffers loss, and all stand to gain sublime contentment.

Young man so dandy and handsome, there is little doubt your success in romance will bring an attractive wife. Yet, bringing a wife in to your home, removes her from the lilting companionship of her sisters and friends. By gaining a consort, others must be bereft. Success in romance is fraught with peaks and valleys. Better by far, to gain success of bodhichitta—where no one suffers heartache, and all stand to gain sublime contentment .

Young man so dandy and handsome, there is little doubt you are a capable horse rider. Though by gaining a swift steed, others must be left behind in the dust. Let your steed be the dharmakaya, and the jockey be focused mindfulness. Better by far, to ride with the wind of spiritual rapture, where no one suffers loss, and all stand to benefit from your attainment.

Thus I sang.

The young man was a good listener, and the words of my song must have affected him. He dismounted, tethered his horse, and came to sit with me.

He asked me about the callous on my hind quarters, and I told him it was something that had come about from long periods of solitary meditation—and would stay with me for the rest of my life.

It started drizzling, but neither of us moved to find shelter. He asked whether higher consciousness could be transferred. I asked that he meditate with me for a while, as the gentle rain continued to fall. When I felt he was ready, I placed the palm of my right hand on his forehead. A few moments later, without an exchange of words, I got up and went on my way up the trail. When I turned to take a parting look, his eyes were shining through his closed eyelids and his smiling countenance was radiant.

Another time, a seeker was convinced I was either an incarnation of Vajrahara Buddha, or that I was a great bodhisattva saint who had attained immeasurable merit over eons. I told the young man, "I honestly didn't know whose incarnation I am. Perhaps I am the incarnation of a being from the lower realms. If you see me as Buddha, then you will receive Buddha's blessing by virtue of your faith. This belief of yours, that I must be an incarnation of a great spiritual being, could be flattering, and is an indication of your devotion to me. However, it could be an impediment to your spiritual development, as it distorts the true dharma."

I went on to tell him that "There is no fault in acknowledging the great achievements of a Buddha or a great bodhisattva. The fault lies in having adulation of me, as a shortcut to your realization. It would be better to see the amazing effectiveness of the dharma. It was the teachings that enabled a great sinner like me to attain results. The dharma, along with renunciation of worldly existence, as well as meditating in seclusion in mountain caves, leads to enlightenment.

"To see me as an incarnation of a great spiritual icon is to dilute the fact that it is possible for every person to achieve what I have achieved. I am living proof that even the worst sinner can attain enlightenment. Put your faith in the law of karma. Be aware of the misery that can arise from worldly existence. Contemplate the lives of great yogis, and keep in mind that no one knows the hour of their death. Devote yourself to the Vajrayana. I deprived myself of food, clothing, and fraternizing. I strengthened my mind and without undue concern for the hardships imposed on my body, I went to meditate in the solitude of the mountains. Over time, the spiritual bliss manifested itself." In that manner, I responded to the boundless enthusiasm of the young seeker.

Thus ends Chapter Nine.

Chapter 10

D URING THE PASSAGE OF SUCCESSIVE YEARS, I meditated at numerous caves—most of which were located along the
north slopes of the mighty Himalayas—which comprise a
watershed for the Tsang valley. Many of my retreats have
been in seclusion, though peppered throughout, there have
been visits by beings from other realms, and human beings
from this world. I had also spent time in the Mount Tisi
region. Known also as Mount Kailas, Tisi is renowned by
Hindus and Buddhists alike as the mother of three mighty
rivers: the Ganges, the Indus, and the Tsampo—which later
become the Brahmaputra.

One time at Mount Tisi, a Bon mystic, who had heard of
my reputation as a holy man, challenged me to a contest. Bon
is the animist religion of Tibet that pre-dated Buddhism. Not
surprisingly, much of Mahayana Buddhism retains Bon esoteric beliefs. Being a powerful mystic, he readily caused fire
to burn in a cave opening where there was no fuel. Another
time, he walked up the side of a large smooth rock—where
even a blue-tongued mountain goat could not go. I took up
the challenge, and flew up and around Mount Tisi—a feat
which he could not match. To prove the height, I struck my
foot upon a prominent rock high up on the cliff face, where
it left a permanent mark.

After decades of wandering, I found myself in the region
of Drin, where there lived a rich and influential lama named

Geshe Tsakpuwa. When he first came seeking an audience, he made a show of honoring me. The next time we met, I could tell he was envious, and wanted to stump me by asking many intellectual questions about the dharma. During the first month of autumn in the year of the Wood Tiger (1135), I had been invited to preside at a wedding taking place at Drin. The Geshe was there also. He came towards me and prostrated himself. I didn't return his prostration, because I had become accustomed to not bowing before anyone in the many years since I had left lama Marpa's compound.

The Geshe was clearly offended. In this, his home region, he was respected outwardly for his wealth and his knowledge of the scriptures, so he expected everyone to prostrate to him. He looked around to the others in attendance, for their acknowledgment of this *faux pas*, but though everyone sensed his embarrassment, no one concurred that he should be bowed to by me. Geshe then produced a thick text on Buddhist logic, and asked whether I would mind going over all its concepts, and explain them in detail.

I knew it was a ruse, and told him that he himself understood the concepts in the text. Indeed, he probably could expound on their intellectual intricacies better than I. I reminded him, and all in attendance, that real spiritual insight is not realized by mastering scripture and text—rather it is found by abandoning worldly attachments, and meditating in mountain solitude. I told him anything I ever knew about logic had probably been forgotten by now—and I wasn't about to start reading pedantic tomes at this latter stage of my life.

The Geshe replied that this may be good enough for a hermit, but if we wanted to compare his knowledge of the scriptural text with mine, he would prevail.

My students were riled at his attitude, and one spoke out, "Lama Geshe, however learned you may be, there are many others like you. You are not the equal of Milarepa—who is unique among men. Please sir, just preside in these ceremonial matters, and do not challenge Master Milarepa."

Chastened, the Geshe looked around, and again saw that he was in a minority of one. It was clear he had been publicly embarrassed, but only he knew what nefarious plan he was hatching in order to gain revenge—against this gaunt pale man, who did not show outward respect for the most important person in the province.

The Geshe went to a private place, and mixed some poison with curdled milk. He promised his mistress a large turquoise, if she were to take the poison drink to a cave in Drin where Milarepa was staying.

When the young woman arrived at my place at the cave, she presented the drink as an offering from the Geshe, but I told her to bring it back later, then I would drink it. This was done for various reasons: The first reason is, though I knew it was poison, I was not afraid to die and had accepted that my time was close at hand. By this time, late in my life, I had many followers, and knew that my chief disciples were either already enlightened, or else were on the verge of becoming so. Additionally, I knew the Geshe would not pay her the turquoise after the fact, so sending her back, would increase her chances of getting paid.

Right away the girl worried that her cover was blown. She reported back to the Geshe, and told him that she thought Milarepa was clairvoyant and had seen right through the deception.

Geshe told her that, if Milarepa was clairvoyant, he would have had *her* drink first from the jar. By not demanding that, Milarepa proved he suspected nothing. He gave her the turquoise, and prodded her in to returning to the hermit with the drink—and to make sure this time he drinks it.

The girl hesitated to leave, and told Geshe that everyone believes Milarepa is clairvoyant. She then stood firm, and declined to return with the poison drink. Geshe turned on his charm and told her he had read a lot about clairvoyance, and assured her that Milarepa did not fit the description of someone who has such abilities. Noticing her continuing reluctance, Geshe promised that if she did this one deed, he would marry her, and his vast array of possessions would be entrusted to her care.

She mixed some additional poison in the curds, then returned and found me alone. She handed me the jar, and I could tell she was thinking, "The Geshe must be right, Milarepa appears ready to drink the poison right away." As I held the jar, I asked her whether the Geshe had given her the turquoise he promised.

Blushing and overwhelmed with fear, she immediately prostrated before me, and said in a trembling voice, "I do have the turquoise but I beg you, do not drink from the jar. Give it back to me, please!"

I asked her what she was going to do with it. She said she would drink it herself.

There were only the two of us there, and we both knew it was poisonous, though neither had mentioned that word. I told her that I had too much compassion to let her drink it. My mission was complete, and my time on this earth was coming to a close. Now that she had the turquoise, I would drink to satisfy the Geshe's desire, and to be sure that she earned the stone. Regarding his other promise, I told her that he would not actually marry her. I also asked her not to mention this conversation until after my death. I then drank the poison. Other than myself, only the Geshe and his mistress knew that I had drunk the poison, and none of us were talking about it.

I went outside and summoned seekers who I came across, and told them to prepare a ritual feast, and gather everyone who wants to meet me to this place. Those who knew me, and heard this request were perplexed, but complied nevertheless. It seemed odd to them that I, who had always eaten sparingly, if at all, and had been known to shun festivities in favor of seclusion, would call for a grand feast. Even more astounding to them, was my call to spread the word that all benefactors, all seekers, all disciples, and indeed all followers who had ever wished to meet me, should come together at Chuwar to congregate.

People from all walks of life gravitated toward Chuwar. As they gathered in a large outdoor meeting place, I spoke to them about karma, and the innate potential of anyone to achieve realization. During this time, several of the chief disciples, clearly saw the sky fill with images of the deities listening to the teachings. Everyone witnessed a rainbow colored canopy appear in the sky—which framed the gathering like a giant luminous tent.

Many in attendance witnessed translucent parasols appearing as apparitions, and a rain of flowers in five colors daintily fell on the assembly. Many also heard celestial music, and beheld the fragrance of frangipani and jasmine—all manifesting spontaneously out of the ether.

Those in attendance were filled with joy, and asked me why they were seeing and experiencing such wondrous things. Upon hearing the comments of their fellow brethren, some asked why certain people could perceive the wondrous signs as tangible, whereas others merely sensed them.

I told them that a person needs subtle vision to see deities, or else one needs intense yearning for virtue and awareness, and a mind unstained by delusion or defilement. Those who are able to clearly see celestial beings, are also able to see their consorts. Additionally, they see the cosmic nature of their own minds, which is the ultimate deity. Then I sang a song called, "How to See Deities."

> Celestial listeners come from the joyful realm of the deities to fill the boundless sky, and to hear the words spoken by the monk Milarepa. Those who possess clear vision see the deities, but common folk see only their celestial offerings.
>
> The sky is filled with rainbow and light, a shower of celestial blossoms falls.
>
> Fragrant frangipani fills the air, and celestial music resounds. Joy and happiness infuse all who are present. Those of you who wish to see the deities and dakinis, tune in to spiritual awareness, which exists within each of you.

Thus sang Milarepa.

And so on that memorable day, the most spiritually developed in attendance realized the true meaning of the Dharmakaya. The less highly developed, experienced awareness in a lucid and joyful way, and set upon the path of enlightenment. Even among the least developed spiritually, there was not one person who did not embrace the practice of Bodhichitta.

It so happened that there were devotees from several regions in attendance. A general sense developed that Milarepa was about to depart this world. That prompted a group of devotees from Nyanang province to insist that, if he were to depart, he should do so from Nyanang. Similarly, a group of devotees from Dingri, felt just as strongly that he should depart from their region. In their zeal, one group clasped hold of one of his legs, while the other group clasped hold of his other, and in this way he was compelled to tell them, "I am old and I will go neither to Nyanang nor to Dingri. Instead, I will wait for my death here. But let go of my legs and stop this foolishness. Regardless of where I die, we will meet again in the Buddha's Pure Land.

The festival and feast lasted many hours. A few days later, Milarepa began showing signs of illness. Several of his closest disciples were gathered around, and offered to perform intense rituals in order to drive away their master's symptoms, but he dissuaded them saying, "I have survived eighty-four cycles of seasons, and am ready to face death. And because I have performed all rituals in accordance with the instructions of lama Marpa, there is no need for ceremonies, rites, drum calls or chanting upon my death. Neither will there be a need to mold ceremonial figurines from the dust of my bones. Evil spirits, who at first appeared menacingly before me, have either been subdued, or have been transformed into protectors of dharma. Neither do I want nor need medicinal herbs or remedies."

Milarepa went on to say, "Now that my time has come, my earthly body has transformed in to a subtle form, and is dissolving into a totally awakened state of emptiness."

About that time, the Geshe showed up and offered Milarepa some meat and beer, and under a thinly-veiled pretense of caring, he inquired about the master's health, saying, "It is a pity that such an illness befalls a saint like master Milarepa. If it were possible to share it, divide it among your disciples. If there were a way to transfer it, then give it to me. Since that is impossible, what then should be done?"

Milarepa smiled and said, "You know very well that my illness has no natural cause. In any case, illness in an ordinary man is not the same as illness in a spiritually attained man. I accept it as an opportunity to transform consciousness to ever higher planes. This sickness enables me to see clearly that samsara and nirvana are, in essence, one reality. It is like an ornament which I mark with the great seal of emptiness— and thereby enables perception of ultimate reality, and blissful awareness. This sickness becomes me. I could transfer it, but I choose not to."

The Geshe suspected that Milarepa knew he gave him the poison, but decided to try to maintain the illusion of innocence and concern, saying, "If I knew the source of the master's sickness, I would exorcize it. Were it a physical disorder, I would find a cure. But I do not know what ails you, so if you can transfer it to me, go ahead."

Milarepa replied, "There is a certain being in this room who is possessed by egotism. It is he who has caused my illness. Geshe, you could neither exorcize this pain, nor cure me. If I were to transfer my illness, you could not bear it for an instant."

The Geshe again asked Milarepa to transfer it—if he could.

Milarepa said, "Well then, I will transfer it to that wooden door. Observe."

Just then there was a loud crack and, shaking violently, the door began to split and break apart. At that same moment, Milarepa was without pain.

The Geshe was awed, but suspected it was a magician's trick, so he asked Milarepa again to transfer it to him.

Milarepa then opted to transfer a bit of the sickness from the door to the Geshe. The Geshe immediately collapsed, paralyzed and choking, writhing on the floor in so much pain he couldn't even call out. Milarepa then withdrew the sickness from him.

Geshe then threw himself at the Master's feet. He admitted his foul plan and begged forgiveness for the evil he had done. He offered his house, and all his wealth to Milarepa, and begged for freedom from samsara—all the while sobbing and praising the master as a great saint.

Milarepa grinned as he responded, "My entire life I have had no desire for house or wealth. Now that I am approaching death, I certainly have no need for them." He then sang a song for the people assembled,

I prostrate myself at the feet of Marpa, the enlightened
   one.

May the sins of all beings be wiped away by the virtue
   of my merits, and those of the Buddhas of the three
   yugas.

May the consequences of this man's karma be assumed
   and transformed by me. In all times and circumstanc-
   es, may he avoid the company of the sinful. In future
   lifetimes, may he meet with virtuous beings.

May he avoid harmful thoughts. May he refrain from
   harming others. May all attain Bodhichitta.

Thus sang Milarepa.

Upon hearing those words, the Geshe was relieved. From
that time on, he pledged to never do anything contrary to the
dharma, but instead would meditate diligently. He admitted
to lying and cheating in the pursuit of wealth, and further
pledged to donate the full value of his property to Milarepa's
disciples. These were accepted, and the proceeds for their
sale were subsequently used during annual ceremonies at
Chuwar, to commemorate Milarepa's death.

Milarepa then decided to travel to a familiar cave at
Chuwar. The disciples were concerned for his failing health,
and offered to fashion a palanquin with which to carry him.
Milarepa waved that idea away, and insisted on traveling
on foot. Some disciples went ahead to the cave, while others
were situated at other caves in the region, not quite knowing the latest news of Milarepa. At a later time, when stories
among disciples were compared one to another, it became
evident that each disciple, whether in a group or in solitary

retreat, communed with Milarepa as though he was directly there with them in person.

Even lay people, who happened to be making offerings in the privacy of their homes, each experienced a personal visit by Milarepa. Also at that time, wonderful colored patterns appeared in the sky. Devout followers say rainbow forms criss-crossed the sky throughout the region. More spiritually attained devotees, saw distinct multi-colored and multi-dimensional mandalas manifest from horizon to horizon.

Thus, this story ends.

A contemporary Tibetan Rinpoche, Lama Tharchin,
who is a friend of the author and is based near Santa Cruz, California.
The word "rinpoche" is an esteemed appellation
which means "incarnate lama" in Tibetan.

Glossary

TIBETAN BUDDHISM has had much influence from India and, to a lesser extent, from Nepal. Because of that, there are many Sanskrit words used when discussing Buddhism. Here is a brief primer of some of the words used within this text:

bodhichitta: immersed in compassion and other heightening spiritual qualities: to awaken the enlightened mind.

Bodhisattva: renunciate monk who adheres to bodhichitta precepts.

chorten: Tibetan for "stupa," meaning a religious structure, usually with a round, wide base rising to a pointed pillar.

dakini: female apparition(s), usually with a lovely blue-colored skin and adorned with jewels; Christians would call them "angels."

Dharma: the Buddhist teachings; one's particular spiritual path.

Dharmakaya: the sublime spiritual experience.

dzo: a cross between a cow and a yak.

fire of Tummo: a specific spiritual practice wherein body temperature noticeably warms.

Geshe: Tibetan for "learned teacher."

gopi: milkmaid.

Guru: teacher.

karma: the rule of cause and effect.

la: Tibetan for "passage" or "pathway."

Lama: Tibetan word for teacher.

Mahamudra: a combination of tantric disciplines that can lead to deep spiritual insight and awareness.

Mahayana: one of two basic paths of Buddhist doctrine; also referred to as "the greater path." Another path is "Hinayana," the lesser path—though the words "greater" and "lesser" indicate a philosophical bent, and are not indicative of one person being better than another.

mara: negative or dark energy.

maha: prefix meaning great, imposing.

nirvana: spiritual rapture.

Rinpoche: Tibetan for an reincarnated teacher.

samsara: bad karma.

Sangha: the community of Buddhist followers.

tantra: advanced Buddhist teachings and practices; the adjective is "tantric."

tsampa: roasted barley meal.

Triple Refuge: the name of a brief invocation which articulates the three things which guide a Buddhist's thoughts and actions to higher levels—the Buddha, Dharma, and Sangha.

SIX-LINE REFUGE PRAYER
(Said while doing prostrations)

Palden lama dam pa nam la kyab su chio
Yidam kyil khor gyi lha tsog nam la kyab su chio
Sang gye chom den de nam la kyab su chio
Dam pai chö nam la kyab su chio
Pag pai gen dun nam la kyab su chio
Pa wo kha dro chö kyong sung mai tsog yeshe kyi
    chen dang den pa nam la kyab su chio

Within all accomplished Lamas, we seek refuge,
Within yidams and deities of the mandala, we seek refuge,
Within transcendent Buddhas, we seek refuge,
Within the supreme Dharma, we seek refuge,
Within the noble Sangha, we seek refuge,
Within dakas, dakinis, and protectors of the dharma, who are
    immersed in enlightened awareness, we seek refuge.

vajra: symbolic artifact, usually hand-held, which is infused with spiritual energy; the Tibetan equivalent is dorje.

Vajrahara: primordial Buddha; used to refer to an enlightened being who exemplifies the basic tenets of Buddhism.

Vajrayana: a series of practices within Mahayana Buddhism, closely lnked to tantra.

yidam: cosmic symbol, of which there are many.

yogi: a seeker, or a practitioner of religion; the female version is yogini.

yuga: an epoch or very long period of time.

About the Author

K EN ALBERTSEN is an American who moved to northern-most Thailand in 1998. Besides writing books (Adventure1.com), he has developed orchards specializing in fruits and nuts not already available in Southeast Asia. Another ongoing project is developing a meditation and cleansing retreat on five secluded acres—with rock climbing crags near the tourist town of Chiang Rai. Other books by Ken: *Homesteading in Thailand, Fasting for Your Health and Your Highness, A1 Idioms Dictionary,* and a novel titled, *Lali's Passage.*

To persuse other books written by Ken, check out
Adventure1.com/store.htm

Enlightened singer of spiritual poems, Milarepa roamed the slopes of Tibet's Himalayas 900 years ago.

"I really enjoyed the audio book. The story is so grounded in simple human reflection. It had a sobering effect on me to perceive of such a larger-than-life character such as Milarepa having such simple problems like me, and be perplexed like me. It made me laugh and let go in some ways."
—Gabriel Lopez, Seattle

4-hour audio recording read by the author
price $10; available from Blue Dolphin Publishing

CPSIA information can be obtained at www.ICGtesting.com
Printed in the USA
LVOW042133170712

290527LV00001B/136/P